TIME

TIME

Daniel Humphrey

ISBN: 978-1-7336598-2-6 (print)
ISBN: 978-1-7336598-3-3 (e-book)

CHAPTER 1

The first thing I remember is the rain—cold, heavy rain-drops pelting my face as I slowly faded into conscious-ness.

Head turned, I blinked my eyes open. A steady bar-rage of raindrops splashed against the pavement in front of my eyes in the blurred daylight. I pushed myself up-right and found myself sitting in the middle of a residen-tial road. I could feel something warm leaking out of my nostrils, running down my chin. I wiped my mouth with the side of my thumb and examined the bright red smear on my shaking hand.

Blood.

What happened to me?

Still in a daze, I rose slowly. Dizziness overwhelmed me. My stomach clenched with nausea. My head was pounding like a war drum. I rubbed the back of my head and rotated in a slow circle, taking in my surroundings. Houses, mailboxes, parked cars, trees dressed in orange and yellow, telephone poles, a fire hydrant, an empty baseball field in the distance.

Where am I?

I staggered toward a dull-blue sedan parked in the street. When I reached the car, I crouched down low and gazed at my reflection in the rain-splattered side-view mirror. A strange feeling came over me, like I was looking at myself for the first time. I had pale skin, brown eyes, and a clean-shaven face. My hair was longer on top—curly and black. A few clumps of my bangs drooped past my eyebrows due to being wet from the rain. I wiped the blood that was still dripping from my nose with the sleeve of the striped sweater I didn't remember putting on. Then I leaned back against the car door and slid down, wincing as I moved my hands to my head.

It was the weirdest phenomenon. I could identify everything around me, and yet I didn't know where I had come from, how I had arrived here, or why I felt so sick, like I had just stepped off a crazy-intense roller coaster. Had I even been on a roller coaster? I could picture one in my head with steel tracks, steep hills, vertical loops, corkscrews, a snake-like vehicle transporting passengers around a circuit. But I had no recollection of riding one or even going to an amusement park.

I tried to gather the thoughts spinning around in my head like a hurricane, retrieve the lost memories surely lurking in my mind somewhere. Any hope that they'd magically appear in the moment was dashed. My brain was a scattered mess of blurry images and emotional chaos. Confusion. Sadness. Fear. Despair. I had no clue what year it was, who my parents were, or if I had any siblings or friends. I didn't even know my own name.

Why can't I remember anything?

I was still reeling, my eyes staring at the white stripes on my Adidas shoes, when I suddenly became aware of some kind of object taking up space in the left front pocket of my pants. I reached inside and pulled out a wallet. Intent on finding some answers, I unfolded it and studied the card in the clear plastic holder, using my hand as an umbrella for the rain.

It was a driver's license. I could comprehend the words on the card. But when did I learn them? The first thing I noticed was the word INDIANA printed in bright orange letters in the top left corner of the card. A black-and-white headshot of me displayed below, with the same curly hair. According to the document, my name was Charlie Benson. I was born on November 29, 2012, and lived on 4674 Ashworth Drive in Barkley, Indiana. None of those facts triggered any recognition in me or filled any of the holes in my memory.

I pulled a navy-blue card from one of the slots, this one a student ID card from Barkley University, issued on June 25, 2031. The name and photo matched the information on the driver's license. If I was in college, I figured I was probably between eighteen and twenty-two years old. So if I was born in 2012, it was probably around 2032 now. I looked again to the trees clothed in bright orange and yellow. Most were still full, with only a few starting to turn bare. Based on that, I guessed the date was sometime around October 2032—give or take a few years. But how did I even know to associate the changing colors of leaves with the month of October? It didn't make any sense, how selective my memory was.

I perused through the remaining cards in the slots and dug out a debit card, a library card, and a green punch card for some smoothie shop. I slid them back in and then opened the pouch for cash and found a twenty-dollar bill inside. I returned my gaze to the address on the driver's license. *That's where I need to go*, I thought. That might lead me to answers more than anything else.

I tucked the wallet back into my pocket as I got to my feet. Still out of it, I started to wander up the road in the unrelenting rain. I picked up the pace to a slow jog. But when I reached an intersection, I stopped.

Wait. Where am I going? I had no idea where 4674 Ashworth Drive was, or if I was even in Indiana.

I heard a low roar behind me. The sound, while muffled in the pouring rain, was growing louder at an alarming rate and increasing in pitch.

I spun around, fear gripping my chest, and looked in horror as an oncoming SUV came hurtling toward me.

CHAPTER 2

Panic shot through me. The car's headlights nearly blinded me. I snapped out of my daze and frantically jumped to the side of the road as the car violently swerved before making a sharp left turn at the intersection, the tires screeching as the vehicle sped off.

I sat on the curb and tried to process what had just happened. The driver must have been in a hurry and didn't see me in the rain until it was almost too late. I guess that's what I get for standing in the middle of an operating road when it's raining.

The rain had soaked through my clothes, leaving me cold and drenched. I needed to find shelter. I got up and started walking again, this time taking the sidewalk, and turned right at the intersection in the opposite direction as the car. The nausea was finally starting to subside a bit, but the dark, uneasy feeling in my bones had only grown stronger since waking up in this confusing yet strangely familiar world.

A few more cars drove by, their windshield wipers sweeping back and forth. I spotted a laundromat and gas station in the distance on opposite sides of the street. The laundromat looked slightly closer, even though it was on the other side of the street, so I headed there.

After crossing the street, I pulled open the door and stepped inside, surrounded by warm, humid air. The overhead fluorescent lights flickered as I took a step forward. The place was empty except for a tall college-looking dude standing behind the counter at the snack bar. He had dark brown hair, and when we made eye contact, the guy smiled and nodded at me.

"Hey," he said, his voice sunny and cheerful, in contrast to the dismal weather outside. His smile faded as soon as he saw the blood on my face and shirt, replaced with a look of concern. "Whoa," he said, taking a step back. "Are you okay, man?"

I hesitated. "I don't know," I finally said, the sound of my voice echoing in my head. It was shaky and weak, laced with anxiety. "I guess...I guess not really?"

"You need to go to the hospital?"

I shook my head. "No," I said, wiping my nose again.

He tore off a paper towel from the roll by the sink and rushed over to me. "Here, use this," he said, offering the paper towel to me.

I grabbed it and started to pack my nose with it.

"Actually, you might want to pinch your nose with it."

"Huh?"

"Like this." He pinched his nose with his thumb and index finger.

I followed suit, squeezing the soft part of my nose, just above my nostrils, with the paper towel—using it to catch the blood.

"Make sure to lean forward," he said, "and just keep holding pressure like that for a while."

As I waited for my nose to stop bleeding, I looked around the room. The shiny floor was lined with various washing machines and dryers, with several laundry carts and folding tables scattered throughout the room. A few small TVs were showing cartoons and highlights from a football game. *Football*, I thought. Did I play football?

After a few minutes, I let go of my nose and inspected the paper towel, which was blotted with dried blood.

"You good?" the guy asked.

I wiped my nose once more. "Yeah, I think so."

"I used to get nosebleeds all the time as a kid," the guy said. "Probably from allergies. Or from picking my nose too much." He smiled. "I'm just kidding...I didn't really have allergies."

Under different circumstances, I might have laughed. Instead, I just stared blankly at him.

"Sorry, bad joke," he said nervously. He held out a hand. "I'm Ollie. Nice to meet you." He waited, clearly wanting to shake hands.

"Um, Charlie," I said, ignoring his hand. I wasn't trying to be rude, but I was still distraught.

Ollie awkwardly pulled his hand back. "So, uh, what happened?" he asked. "I mean, if you don't mind me asking."

"I, um, I don't really know," I said, struggling to keep my voice even. "I woke up in the middle of the road in the rain, and I don't really remember anything before that."

"Oh," he said, taking it in. "So what do you think happened?"

"I have no idea."

"Did you…have any alcohol?"

I shook my head. "No, I don't drink," I quickly said. But how did I know that? Then a disturbing thought struck me.

Could I have been drugged?

"Okay, but you have to admit, you can see how this looks, right?" Ollie said. "A guy who looks like he's in college wakes up in the middle of the road with no memory of how he got there and a bloody nose."

"You think I'm lying?"

"No, no, no. I'm sorry. Okay, let's just take a breather. I'm just—I'm trying to make sense of this all. This is very new to me." He paused. "So what's the last thing you remember before waking up?"

"I don't remember anything, man."

"It doesn't have to be, like, from today or last night. What about last week? Or last month?"

I shook my head. "Nothing, man."

His mouth dropped. "So you really don't remember anything?"

I nodded. "I mean, I know how to read. And I know that one plus one is two. But other than that, it's like my memory's been erased. And when I woke up, I got this weird feeling like...like I was...planted here or something."

He looked at me strangely, like he was trying to read me. "Were you sent from outer space for a mission? Is your spaceship floating around somewhere?"

"No," I said flatly. "It's parked on the ground, actually."

He shot me a confused look, then glanced out the window into the parking lot.

"I'm joking," I said.

He smiled, then laughed. "That's a dangerous game, man."

I smiled for just a moment, but then the reality of my situation sank in again, and sadness washed over me.

"But, hey, maybe it's a good thing you don't remember everything," Ollie continued, probably trying to cheer me up. "I mean, everyone has things they wish they could forget." He paused. "I'm sorry. That was really insensitive. I find it hard when I forget where I parked at the mall, so I can't imagine how that feels. You must be scared."

I nodded, once again reminded of it all. A lump formed in my throat. But I just shrugged, not saying anything.

A few seconds of silence passed.

"Do you want me to go call someone for you?" Ollie asked, breaking the silence. "Like a friend or family member or something?"

I hesitated, then shook my head slightly. "I can't remember anyone."

"Oh. Right."

The silence returned. Then I suddenly remembered the address from the driver's license in my pocket. "Hey, are we in Barkley, Indiana?" I asked.

Ollie nodded. "Yeah."

I quietly sighed in relief. "Do you know where Ashworth Drive is?"

"Yeah, I think it's over by Hayward."

"Hayward?"

"Hayward Fieldhouse. It's where Barkley plays basketball."

"Thanks." I turned around and started toward the door.

"Wait," Ollie said. "Where are you going?"

"I need to go there."

"I really think you should go to the hospital, man."

"I'm fine." I kept walking, but Ollie chased after me. When he caught up to me, he reached into his pocket and slipped out a wallet, then opened it and pulled out a one-dollar bill and a quarter.

"Here," he said, offering me the money. "There's a bus stop right up the street." He eyed the clock on the wall. "The next bus arrives in, like, fifteen minutes. You can use this to pay the fare."

"No, no, I can't."

"You expect to get there on foot in the rain? In your condition? Just take it."

"I have a twenty."

He shook his head. "They won't accept a twenty. You need exact change." He extended his arm. "Just take it, man."

I hesitated, then finally took the cash. "Thanks, man. You really don't have to do this."

"Yeah, well, you won't go to the hospital, and it doesn't cost a cent to be decent, right?" He paused. "Well, in this case, I guess it costs a dollar twenty-five, so maybe that's a bad example, but you get the point."

We stood in silence until, a few seconds later, Ollie walked back to the counter. "One more thing." He grabbed a pencil and started to jot something down on a sticky note. When he finished, he ripped off the note and handed it to me. "Here's my number, so you can call me whenever, you know, since I'm pretty much the only person you know right now." He paused. "Good luck. I hope you get your memory back."

"Thank you."

I folded the sticky note and stuffed it into my pocket, then headed outside and found a blue-and-green bus stop sign on a nearby metal pole. I sat down on the bench in the shelter. Fear and worry rose up inside me as I waited, almost too much to bear. I took a deep breath and tried to force myself to calm down and accept the situation. *Everything will be okay*, I told myself. *Just be patient, and the answers will come.*

The bus pulled up with a squeal. I waited for one of the passengers to exit before climbing onto the bus.

"Afternoon," the bus driver—a bald black guy—said to me.

"Hey," I said, looking at the machine in front of me.

"First time?" the driver asked.

I nodded. "Yeah."

"Pass or cash?"

"Uh, cash," I said, holding up the money Ollie had given me.

He pointed to a slot on the right side of the machine. "Dollar bills go in the top one there, and coins go in the one below it."

I slipped the quarter and one-dollar bill into the appropriate slots, then thanked the driver and found a seat. A few other passengers were scattered throughout the bus.

As the bus rolled out, I turned my head and watched as two raindrops raced down the window. I tried to guess which one was going to win. One joined with another raindrop and suddenly picked up speed, like a speed boost in a video game. The mega-raindrop won, which didn't seem fair since it had cheated. I kept watching, hoping the little dots in my head would soon connect like the raindrops sliding down the window.

Eventually, my eyes drifted beyond the window to look at my surroundings as the world went by, trying to see if anything looked familiar. I understood what the buildings sliding past were for—stores, restaurants, and hotels, for example—but I didn't remember ever visiting or even seeing any of them before, like I was traveling to a new city for the first time.

I kept an eye on the locations scrolling across the LED sign at the front of the bus. When I saw my stop approaching, I signaled the driver by pulling the yellow cord at the top of the window next to me.

The bus pulled up to the curb. I thanked the driver before stepping off. The rain had relented to a drizzle, painting the air with a misty haze. I gazed at the huge brick arena nearby. That must be Hayward Fieldhouse, I thought. If Ollie was right, I was close. Close to seeing my family. Close to getting some answers. Close to being home.

I shifted my eyes to an intersection and saw two green

street signs hanging on a light pole. One of them read SARATOGA RD, and the other one read ASHWORTH DR. I headed toward the signs, passing several trees along the way—their vibrant leaves shining like a bright light on a hilltop. But when I looked out at Ashworth Drive, I stopped and felt my heart drop.

The road was empty, except for a few houses still in the early phases of construction. Instead of houses lining the street, vacant lots and fields of grass occupied the open space.

I checked the street signs again to make sure I was in the right area. I looked for addresses on the houses being built, even scanned the ones on Saratoga Road, just in case. But eventually, I faced reality.

The address on my driver's license didn't exist.

CHAPTER 3

Nothing made any sense. I tried to run through the possibilities in my head but came up empty. My thoughts were tangled, twisted fears. Maybe Ollie had been on to something. Maybe I *was* an alien from outer space planted on earth for a mission. Whatever my mission was, I was definitely failing—unless my mission was to get a bloody nose, almost get hit by a car, or go sightsee some vacant lots. It was like someone was playing a cruel and elaborate prank on me. I just wanted for all of this to end.

Well, now what?

I had nowhere to go, so I started to wander back toward the bus stop. On the way there, I saw an underpass up ahead with a paved bike trail running through it. I figured the underpass would provide shelter from the rain, so I started walking along the bike path.

When I reached the underpass, I walked up the concrete slope next to the trail and sat down at the top, leaning my back against the wall. My head was only a few feet from the road above me, and I could hear cars whizzing by overhead.

For some reason, I slipped out the sticky note in my pocket with Ollie's phone number on it. If I called him—which I couldn't, because I didn't have a phone—and told him about the nonexistent address on my driver's license, it would be straight to the hospital with a bunch of brain scans. And a bunch of huge bills. And still possibly no real answers.

I slipped the note back into my pocket and pulled out my wallet again. I took out my student ID and studied it. I was apparently a student at Barkley University. Ollie had told me that Ashworth Drive was close to the arena where Barkley's basketball team played. That meant I had to be close to the campus. Shouldn't this area be familiar, then? I looked around at the nearby buildings and kept telling myself to try to remember. But it was like driving down memory lane in dense fog.

I remember...nothing.

I leaned forward, rested my elbows on my knees, and hung my head. I stayed like that for a while until I heard a now-familiar voice from below say, "Hey!"

I looked down, and there was Ollie in front of me, standing on the trail.

"How's it going?" he asked.

"Okay."

"Did you find the address you were looking for?"

"Yeah, um, sort of," I said, not wanting to tell him that the address didn't exist.

"What are you doing out here?"

"I could ask you the same thing."

"Oh, I was just…jogging," he said, even though it was obvious from his jeans and Vans that he had not been jogging. He paused. "Okay, I lied," he admitted. "I wasn't actually running. To tell you the truth, I was on my way back from work when I saw you, and you looked kind of lost, so I wanted to check on you and see if you needed any help."

"I'm good, thanks."

"You sure you don't want me to take you to the hospital? There's one not far from here."

"Yeah, I'm sure."

"Well, do you have a place to stay?"

"Yeah," I lied.

"Doesn't look like you do."

I didn't say anything. Instead, I nervously fidgeted with my student ID, but then it suddenly slipped out of my fingers and slid all the way down the slope, stopping at Ollie's feet. He picked up the card and glanced at it.

"Whoa!" he said, his face lighting up. "You go to Barkley University? Why didn't you tell me? That's where I go!" He ran up the slope and handed me the card. "I'm a sophomore acting major. What year are you?"

"I don't know."

"If you're a fellow student, then I should help you. What's your major?"

"Yeah, um, I have no idea."

"Do you know if you live on campus?"

I shook my head.

Ollie stood there for a second, then said, "Come with me. I'll show you the dorm I live in and introduce you to some of the residents. It's not far from here. We can walk there."

I thought for a moment. From what I could tell, Ollie seemed like a genuine dude. I mean, he'd been nothing but nice to me since I'd stumbled into the laundromat with a bloody nose. Plus, maybe exploring the campus would bring back memories of being a college student.

When I stood up, Ollie gave a satisfied nod. "Come on, let's go," he said, walking in the same direction he had come from. I waited for a few seconds and then followed. We walked up a small hill and came to an intersection with a stoplight.

As we waited to cross the street, Ollie turned to me. "You know, I used to keep a journal when I was a kid," he said, which seemed completely random to me. He smiled. "I know, real gangster of me, right? I used to think I was so slick, writing in my own private journal. I even had a lock and key to open it." He shook his head and let out a small laugh. "I don't know why. Most of the stuff I wrote in it was just what food I ate that day." He paused. "Anyway, one day I lost the key to the lock and couldn't open it. I was so upset. My mom ended up finding the key a few days later. And you know where it was?"

"No, where?" I said, trying to move him along.

"Turns out, it was in my pocket the whole time. She found it when she was doing laundry. Can you believe that?"

"That's crazy," I said, still wondering where he was going with this.

"Yeah, I know, right? Anyway, what I'm trying to say is…this won't last forever. Your memories are there. Locked away somewhere. We just have to find the key."

I looked at him. "We?"

"Sure. Look, I don't know if you're a glass-half-full kind of guy or glass-half-empty, you know, but I'm gonna help you get through this, Charlie. Okay? We're gonna figure it out."

Something was telling me that Ollie was a glass-half-full kind of guy. I didn't get why he was being so nice to me—a random, possibly insane (or even extraterrestrial) stranger. But I appreciated his kindness and concern, nonetheless.

"Thank you, Ollie."

The brick dorm building looked older than I had expected. "So, is this it, Ollie?"

"Yep, this is it. Reinhart Hall. Or as I like to call it, Die-Hard Hall."

"Die-Hard?"

"Yeah. There have been a lot of rumblings of this place getting demolished, and yet it still continues to stand in spite of all that. To be honest, I'll be sad to see it go. It's a piece of Barkley history."

It's a piece of something, I thought. But I kept my thoughts to myself.

Ollie looked proudly up at the building in front of us. "It's old, but it's home. She's still got it going on, you know? I mean, it's outdated, but charming, in a way. Trashy, but classy, if you know what I mean."

I had no idea what he meant.

I could only stand there and gawk at it. I know my memory was kind of fuzzy, to say the least, but I doubted I'd ever seen such an old building. The four-story structure looked like it had been built at least a century ago.

There was a wide walkway with a small set of steps in front of the building. Bike racks sat on both sides of the walkway, partially filled. Four white pillars stood at the top of the steps, supporting a narrow flimsy-looking deck. A small white bell tower rose above the roof.

"There have also been a lot of rumors about this place being haunted," Ollie went on.

"What do you mean?"

"Oh, you know, the usual stuff. Strange noises, flickering lights. There's this one legend about a girl who supposedly died in the basement or went missing and never returned, and how her ghost haunts the walls within the building." He paused. "Well, shall we go inside?"

On that pleasant note...

A few stray leaves crunched under my feet as Ollie guided me toward the entrance of the dorm building. A large unlit lantern hung over the wooden door. The worn white paint on the door was shedding like a snake's skin.

After going through the first door, there was a second door requiring key-card entry. Ollie waved his ID card in front of a scanner, and when I heard a click, I pulled the door open and headed inside with Ollie.

A stale, musty smell invaded my senses as soon as I stepped inside, only adding to the creepy feel of the building. The place was just as old-fashioned and spooky on the inside. The walls were a stingy whitish-yellow color. Narrow hallways with arched entries stretched in every direction.

Ollie told me to turn right. As I turned, Ollie waved at a young black guy with glasses sitting at the front desk.

"What's up, Ronnie?" he said to him.

Ronnie nodded at him. "Hey, Ollie, what's good?"

"That's Ronnie," Ollie said to me. "He lives on my floor. He's cool. I'll introduce you to some of the others, too."

Ollie led me to a stairwell and told me that he lived on the top floor. We headed up. The stairwell had windows made of glass blocks—the kind that lets in light but you can't see through. Not much light was coming in though with the overcast weather and the sun starting to set.

"I'm not gonna lie," Ollie said on the way up, "these stairs are pretty annoying sometimes, especially in August and September, when it's still really hot outside. There's no AC in the stairwell, and the sun beats down on you through the glass. You can't even go up the stairs without working up a sweat, especially if you're wearing a backpack."

I heard voices as I reached the top of the steps. Then laughter. We started down the long hallway past the pale-blue walls. Music drifted from one of the rooms. A dozen or so dudes of all shapes and sizes were gathered in a common area by the bathroom, engaging in some kind of spirited debate. But when they saw us, they stopped debating and greeted Ollie. Some of them looked curiously at me.

Ollie introduced me to everyone in the common area. A Korean computer science major named Suehan. A skinny blond dude from Wisconsin majoring in math. A shorter guy from Vietnam majoring in chemical engineering. And plenty more. Ollie didn't tell them about my situation, and neither did I. I wanted to keep it under wraps as much as possible.

Ollie's dorm room happened to be right by where the group of residents were gathered. He took out a dull golden key and inserted it into the keyhole on the door. After opening the door, he walked across the tile floor and opened the window, letting in fresh air. I guess the rain had finally stopped. I stood in the doorway.

"You can come in, man," Ollie said to me. "Welcome to my humble abode."

I stepped inside and scanned the room. The room was larger than I had expected. A single long two-person desk lined the wall in front of the door. The shelves mounted on top were filled with books and other items. A small TV sat in the middle of the desk, between the two chairs. An unzipped backpack hung from one of the chairs, with more books and notebooks hanging out. A bunk bed stood in the far corner of the room by the window. Only the bottom bunk was fitted with sheets, blankets, a pillow, and a comforter. The top bunk just had a bare mattress. Two navy-blue beanbag chairs sat in front of the bottom bunk. The room also had a built-in closet with sliding doors. Despite its age, the room was nice and clean.

Ollie noticed me looking at his bookshelves. "So this is basically my entire library," he said. He pointed to a portable stereo sitting on the desk. "Boombox is a nice touch, I know." He started sifting through the CDs lined against the wall on the desk. "We got so many great albums here. We got The Killers. We got Switchfoot, Relient K, Coldplay, Lifehouse. So yeah, we're rocking in this dorm room." He paused. "Do you know any of these bands?"

I shook my head.

"Man, I need to assign you some music to listen to as homework, like in *The School of Rock*."

"*The School of Rock*?"

"Yeah. You know, with Jack Black?"

I shook my head again.

"The School...of Rock," Ollie said again, but in a faraway voice this time—looking off in the distance. "And we shall teach rock 'n' roll...to the world." He looked back at me. "Ring any bellzzz?" he said, dragging out the last part of the word and sounding like a bee.

Once again, I shook my head.

Ollie threw his hands up in mock disgust and shook his fists with maximum drama. "Oh, what do they teach in this place?!" he yelled, scaring me a little.

"You okay in there?" a voice called from the hallway.

"That's just Ollie being Ollie," another voice said.

"Sorry," Ollie said, back in his normal voice. "Got a little carried away there. But that was all from the movie. Speaking of movies..." He reached down and grabbed a DVD from a stack next to the CDs. "This is a really great movie called *Surf's Up*, which is about a penguin named Cody Maverick, and he dreams of becoming a pro surfer, and the movie is about him pursuing that."

I looked at the cover and wondered if I had seen that movie and just didn't remember watching it. The cover featured an animated penguin riding a wave on a surfboard, with a few other penguins—and even a chicken—also surfing behind him. "Is it a kid's movie?" I asked.

"Yes, it is, and it's freaking amazing. Or, as a surfer might say, *gnarly.*" He smiled. "If you stick around, man, we gotta have a movie night sometime and watch it."

"I think I might be a little too old for that," I said bluntly.

Ollie looked at me with disappointment. "Well, Charlie, I hear you, and I am going to choose not to be offended by that. Because my goal is to always be my ten-year-old self. I think one of the most important things in life is to never lose your childlike sense of wonder. To keep exploring. Be curious." He paused. "Anyway, this is one of my all-time favorite movies because it's a perfect example of, like, growth and resilience throughout the entire movie. It taught me so much about when you are feeling, like, you know, you're not doing the right thing, or, you know, you're just never going to make it. He perseveres through this, and that really resonates with me and my acting. Sometimes I feel like with acting, I just can't click with it sometimes, and I'm, like, am I really doing the right thing? This movie reminded me that true success comes from within. And that the journey itself is just as important as the destination."

We'd only just met, but I could already see how determined and passionate Ollie was about his acting. I thought back to my student ID and wondered what I was studying, if there was anything I was passionate about.

Ollie shifted his attention to the bottom bookshelf. "Moving on to *la biblioteca*," he said—which I knew meant *library* in Spanish. But again, how did I know that?

"First shelf is all plays," Ollie continued. "I'm a theater kid. So this would be playwrights—you know, Neil Simon, Arthur Miller, Tennessee Williams. So many other great playwrights on this shelf." He paused. "By the way, I'm gonna perform as Dallas Winston in a local production of *The Outsiders*. We open next week at the performing arts theater here on campus. You should totally come watch it, if you're free. I can hook you up with some sweet tickets. Should be fun. It really is a tear-jerker, for sure, and it's just so beautifully written."

He raised his eyes to the next shelf. "Second shelf would be fiction," he said, changing topics. "Novels, basically. *Harry Potter. The Hobbit.* Some great books on that shelf. And then third shelf is non-fiction. This is my entire library, pretty much."

I scanned the row of fiction, trying to find a title I recognized—something to shed light on my foggy past, like feeling the wall for a light switch in the middle of the night. But the titles were all foreign to me. I had no idea whether the books on the shelf were wildly popular books that everyone knows or obscure niche books that only a select few know or care about.

Frustrating, right?

"Oh, I gotta show you my shoe collection," Ollie said with an excited look on his face. He showed me to the closet and then slid the door open. "I have a bunch of shoes in here." He reached down and pulled out a pair of white high-top shoes with a blue Nike swoosh on them. "So, like, I have my Nike Blazers, which I got these like a couple years back—like a year and a half ago. And I really like them." He pulled out another pair of black low-cut shoes. "I got my other Vans here. These are skate shoes. I'm a poser as far as skating goes. I don't really skate, but I do like me some skate shoes. My girlfriend actually got me these for my birthday."

"You have a girlfriend?" I said, without thinking.

He smiled. "Don't act so surprised, man. But yeah. Hope you can meet her sometime."

After Ollie showed me the rest of his shoe collection, I glanced around the room again, then looked at the bunk bed. "So where's your roommate?" I asked.

"I'm actually flying solo. I'm an RA, so they let me have a room to myself."

"You're an RA?"

"Yeah. Resident assistant. It's basically a student staff member who lives and works in a residence hall on campus. We help and mentor the students living on our floor and serve as a resource for them. We get perks, like free housing and a room to ourself, hence the empty bed. These beds were actually both on the floor when I first moved in, but I decided to bunk the beds to create more space." He paused. "You can use the extra bed for the night if you want."

I thought again. I had my reservations earlier, but it was hard to remain skeptical. Everyone I'd met so far, including Ollie, was a little odd, but they'd welcomed me with open arms. Plus, staying here had to be better than sleeping outside.

"You sure?" I said. "I don't want to impose, man."

"Not at all, man. It's the least I can do. I mean, I can't imagine what you're going through. I'll show you a store where you can buy sheets and a pillow tomorrow. You'll have to make do with just my extra blanket for tonight."

"Thank you, man."

"Yeah." He paused. "So…no memories yet?"

I shook my head.

"We'll figure it out. You're going to be okay."

I wished I shared his optimism.

After finishing the tour, I followed Ollie back into the hallway. But when I stepped out, I wasn't paying attention and bumped into Ronnie—the worker from the front desk on the first floor—who was walking past Ollie's door at the same time, knocking the newspaper out of his hand and almost causing both of us to fall.

"My bad, man," Ronnie said to me after regaining his balance. "Didn't see you there."

I picked up the newspaper and was about to take ownership for the collision when I caught a glimpse of the date on the front page.

My heart froze. "Is this…today's newspaper?" I asked, feeling the fear take hold again.

Ronnie nodded. "Yeah. You wanna borrow it?"

I shook my head—more in disbelief than to say no.

The date in the newspaper was October 29, 2008—more than four years before I was even born.

CHAPTER 4

My mind raced. I tried to put it together.

What the heck is going on? It's 2008? No. This isn't happening. I'm dreaming. This has to be a dream. Okay, wake up, Charlie. Wake up right now.

I squeezed my eyes shut, trying to force myself to wake up, but when I opened my eyes, nothing had changed. Ramping up to full-on panic mode, I slapped myself on the cheek a few times, ignoring the looks on the faces of the people around me. *They're not real anyway,* I thought. *This is all just some kind of weird nightmare.* But that didn't work either.

My nausea returned. I needed to sit down. I glanced around the hallway, then stumbled toward a small wood sofa by the bathroom and plopped down.

Ollie came over to me with a look of concern on his face. "Hey. You okay?"

"Yeah," I said, wiping the sweat off my face with my sleeve.

I'm from the future! I wanted to scream, but it wasn't information I was sure I should share with Ollie—or with anyone, for that matter. First of all, because it would make me sound crazy, buying me a one-way trip to the loony bin. Second, I still refused to believe it was true—that I had somehow traveled from the future. I had to be imagining the whole thing, right? There was just no way. But eventually, the shocking reality of my situation began to sink in, and I forced myself to try to accept it and deal with it. At least now the nonexistent address made sense. The house I lived in must not have been built yet.

That was about the only thing that made any sense.

A few hours later, I was lying in the dark on the top bunk in Ollie's dorm room, struggling to fall asleep. Ollie was already snoring in the bed below. But it wasn't his snoring, the hissing of the radiator, or not having proper bed sheets keeping me up. It was the whole, you know, traveling-through-time thing that was bouncing around my brain like crazy. I mean, how could I sleep at a time like this?

I thought about my past life—or, I guess, my future life—and wondered if I ever have trouble sleeping like this in the future. I wondered about my parents, if they were alive in this world. The fact I couldn't remember anything about my life filled my heart with misery, like a dark cloud constantly floating in my chest. I guess memory loss must be a potential side effect of time travel—as well as nausea, dizziness, and a bloody nose. Kind of makes sense, if you think about it—that traveling through time would do a number on someone. In that sense, I was grateful to still be alive, that traveling through time hadn't killed me—at least, not yet. But how did I even get here in the first place? And how do I go back? I silently repeated those questions to the ceiling, but the ceiling, of course, offered no insight whatsoever. Stupid ceiling.

Okay, now I really was starting to go crazy, if I hadn't crossed that threshold already.

The window was still cracked open, letting in cold air—counteracting the heat coming from the radiator. I didn't know if Ollie had forgotten to close it or if he liked having the window open at night. I listened to the sounds coming from the street. Car doors. People talking. Every now and then, a group of rowdy students would drive by, the car speakers spilling out the latest tunes—or, I guess, since I was in the past, they were actually retro tunes, instead. That was pretty weird to think about.

Okay, let's be real. This whole thing was pretty crazy to think about.

I must have dozed off eventually, because when I found myself opening my eyes, it was already light. For a moment, everything felt normal—like just another morning. But then it hit me that I was stuck in the past, and sadness and emptiness pervaded my heart once again.

I climbed quietly down the bunk bed, careful not to wake Ollie. But his bed was empty. I looked at the clock after my feet hit the floor. It was almost noon. Sheesh, I didn't think I had slept that long. My exhaustion from the day before must have caught up to me.

I found a note from Ollie on the desk saying that he had classes in the morning and would be back for lunch. I looked at the clock again. It was probably close to lunchtime.

Sure enough, as if on cue, I heard someone opening the door. I jolted a little, startled, but then relaxed when Ollie opened the door with a big smile on his face. He wore a puffer jacket over a white hoodie, black pants, and one of the Nike shoes he'd shown me the night before.

"Morning, Charlie."

"Hey, uh, good morning," I said, my voice groggy from just waking up.

"How'd you sleep?"

"Um, all right, I guess," I said, rubbing my eyes.

He slipped off his backpack. "So after my last class this morning, I took the liberty of stopping by the administration building." He paused. "Your last name is Benson, right?"

"Yeah," I said, wondering how he knew my last name.

"I saw it on your ID card when you dropped it yesterday," Ollie said, noticing my curious expression.

I tensed up, wondering if he had also seen the issue

date on my ID card. No, I convinced myself. The print was too small. He'd have to really study it like I did to notice it.

"Anyway," Ollie continued, "I asked the staff to search for your name to see if you were registered for any classes or had any relatives listed we could contact. But the weirdest thing happened. It didn't come up in the system. Your name isn't even in the database."

That made sense, I thought, since I was from the future and wouldn't enroll for another twenty-plus years. But, of course, Ollie didn't know that.

"Weird," I said.

"Yeah, right? I also noticed your ID card looked a little different than mine." He paused. "You think…maybe you enrolled at a different Barkley University or something?"

I shrugged. "No clue," I lied.

We fell into silence for a moment or two. Then Ollie said, "Well, you ready for lunch?"

Not really, I thought, while saying, "Sure."

I slipped on my Adidas, and then Ollie grabbed his backpack and led me down the stairs toward the dining hall on the first floor. Ollie explained to me there were three dorm buildings all connected, and the dining hall we were going to was nestled in the middle of them.

As we walked by the front desk, I heard the sound of bells chiming a sequence of musical notes above us.

"What's that sound?" I asked.

"Huh? Oh, that's the bell tower on top of the building," Ollie explained. "It plays, like, every day at noon, I think."

For some reason, the sound of the bells ringing throughout the halls creeped me out a little.

On our way to the dining hall, we walked down a long narrow hallway lined with portraits. I glanced over my shoulder at one of the portraits. It was of a very old white-haired man who looked out from the canvas with dark beady eyes. The eyes had an odd gleam in them. I kept my gaze on the portrait to see if the eyes would follow me as I went past, like in a spooky old mansion. At this point, I wouldn't have been surprised if they did.

"This is actually one of my favorite dining halls on campus," Ollie said as we got closer to the entrance. "And not just because it's convenient, since I live here. It tastes like homestyle cooking. They make real mashed potatoes. It's not just powdered stuff. It's usually with lumps like real mashed potatoes. And their chicken fingers are always really good. And that sauce"—he pinched his fingers and thumb together and did a chef's kiss gesture—"*mwah*, beautiful." He paused. "Also, the tables kind of make you feel like you're at Hogwarts."

"Hogwarts?" I said, confused.

"Yeah. You know, from *Harry Potter*?"

Wait. That name sounded familiar. I got a little excited, thinking I had finally unlocked a concrete memory.

But then I remembered Ollie showcasing his bookshelves the night before and realized it was just from some of the books on his shelves.

"Oh, that's right," Ollie continued, "you don't remember anything. Well, maybe this will jog your memory." He cleared his throat and started speaking in a strange high-pitched voice. "Master has given Dobby a sock. Dobby is *free*."

I just stared at him blankly.

Seeing my confusion, he suddenly switched to a different character, like somebody trying on different shoes to see if any of them would fit. "Yer a wizard, Harry," he said in a gruff voice and with a thick accent. "An' a thumpin' good'un, I'd wager, once yer trained up a little."

I shook my head. "Sorry, no."

"No?" he said, staying in character. "Blimey, Harry! I keep forgettin' how little yeh know—not knowin' about Hogwarts!" He grinned, finally breaking character.

To be honest, I was really impressed—and a little freaked out—by how easily he could morph into different characters. The two voices couldn't have been any more different, and yet they both had felt real and natural. It wasn't just his voice that had changed either. It was his whole countenance. I could tell he definitely had some acting chops, and the passion was clearly there, too.

We walked up to the dining hall checker—an older

Latina woman with shortish brown hair. She wore glasses, and her turquoise oval earrings matched her branded polo shirt. She also wore a white vest over her polo with a bedazzled heart-shaped brooch pinned to it. She greeted us with a warm smile and had a gentle demeanor.

Ollie pulled his student ID from his wallet, and the lady scanned it with this handheld barcode reader.

"How are classes going?" she asked with a bit of an accent.

"Good!" Ollie said. "Starting to get to that busy part in the semester, but going well so far."

She smiled. "Good."

I pulled out my wallet and opened it. Ollie must have had a meal plan with the university. I wondered if I did, too, but even if I did, I knew there was still no chance my current ID card would work since I wasn't even enrolled at the university yet. My ID card and debit card were basically useless here. So I took out the twenty-dollar bill, instead.

"How much for a meal?" I asked nervously.

"Lunch price is twelve-twenty-two."

I swallowed. That was more than half the money I had. I felt an overwhelming sense of urgency. I needed to find a way out of here and head back to my own world pronto.

"You can try scanning your ID card," Ollie said to me. "You might have a meal plan set up."

"That's okay. I'm just gonna use cash." I reluctantly handed the woman the money, and she gave me my change.

"Have a good meal."

"Thank you."

I followed Ollie as other students shuffled in for lunch. There was a sandwich bar on the left and a buffet on the right. I grabbed a plate and made my way through the buffet line, filling my plate with everything Ollie was recommending to me. We then walked through a narrow doorway to the right of the buffet into the main dining hall. I glanced around the room. The walls were covered with vertical wood panels and huge windows that looked out into the campus. Rows of long wooden dining tables seated with other students filled the somewhat cramped space.

We set our plates down on an unoccupied section of the table closest to us and then went to the salad bar and desert bar and got drinks. I settled for orange Gatorade, while Ollie poured a bizarre concoction of various drinks from the soda fountain into a single cup.

"So how're you holding up?" Ollie asked as we took our seats.

I shrugged. "All right, I guess. You know, given the circumstances."

"So I was thinking, maybe we could get the police involved in this? If we take a picture of you, they can get your photo circulated to social media and newspapers and stuff like that. A story like yours—it's big stuff, you know? Like, Eragon-finding-the-blue-egg big. And if we get your face out there, then surely someone's gonna recognize you."

I had no idea what to do here. The fact was, no one would recognize me if a photo of me were to be shared with the public. I hadn't even been born yet. And going to the police would force me to expose my identity, since they'd inevitably go through my belongings, and who knows what would happen after that? I didn't want to find out.

I guess I could just chuck my wallet before going to the police, but my wallet was the only thing I had with me from my past...or, future. Whatever. My main concern right now was recovering my memory. And finding a way back to my own world. I figured the two probably went hand in hand. If I could remember how I got here— how I traveled to the past—then I could most likely find a way back.

"I don't think that's a good idea," I said.

"Why not?"

I said nothing.

Ollie looked at me skeptically. "Okay, be straight with me, man. Are you on the run or something?"

"No," I said quickly. At least, I didn't think so. But really, who was to say?

"I mean, I'd already be an accomplice at this point, so you can be honest with me. I just wanna know if I should lawyer up."

I debated how to tiptoe around the truth. I couldn't tell him all of it. He'd probably never believe it anyway. Heck, I still wasn't sure if I even believed it. But I had to convince him that I wasn't a fugitive without telling him the whole truth.

"I know I don't have any solid memories at the moment," I said, "but..."

But what? How could I possibly convince him that I wasn't a fugitive when I didn't even know for sure that I wasn't?

"Uh, speaking of repressed memories..." Ollie said, changing the subject—much to my relief. He reached down and dug out a thick textbook from his backpack. "My girlfriend's taking a psych class, and I stole her textbook from her. Actually, I didn't steal it. She let me borrow it. I don't know why I said that." He opened the textbook and started flipping through the pages. "Anyway, in this book, there's a chapter about how to retrieve memory through triggers, like, you know, taste and smell and touch." He stopped flipping and pushed my plate closer to me. "Okay, close your eyes."

"Why?"

"Just do it."

I closed my eyes.

"Okay, now grab a chicken finger."

"But I can't see anything."

"Fine," he said with a sigh. "Open your eyes."

I opened my eyes.

"Now grab a chicken finger."

I grabbed a chicken finger.

"And dip it in the sauce."

I dunked the chicken finger into the mystery dipping sauce—a sort of orange or beige color.

"Now close your eyes again."

"I already know it's a chicken finger."

"Yeah, but the smell could be a trigger."

I closed my eyes. The smell of chicken hit me, and I suddenly realized that I was starving.

"What are you smelling right now?"

"Uh…chicken."

"Is the smell taking you back?"

I moved the chicken finger closer to my nose and took another whiff. "Not really," I said, shaking my head.

"Well, take a bite. Let the sauce work its magic."

I took a bite and started to chew. The chicken was crispy and juicy on the inside. The sauce had a slight kick to it—creamy and tangy—and paired well with the chicken.

"Okay," Ollie said. "Now really think about past meals you've had. Do you remember ever eating chicken fingers?"

I swallowed and shook my head. "I mean, it's good, but it's not really taking me back."

"Okay, okay, dump the chicken. Try the mashed potatoes."

I grabbed my fork and took a bite of the mashed potatoes. The texture was mostly smooth, with some small lumps throughout. I liked the flavor. It was creamy and buttery with a hint of black pepper. But it still wasn't evoking any kind of recollections.

"I don't think this is working," I said to Ollie. I was about to take another bite anyway when I saw the checker from the entrance heading toward me.

And she was carrying my wallet—with my IDs from the future.

CHAPTER 5

I tried not to panic. Did she see my birthdate on my driver's license? Or the issue date on my student ID? If so, then what would happen? How could I explain that to her? I ran my hands along the sides of my pants, both to feel for my wallet in case I was mistaken and to wipe off the sweat that was quickly forming on my hands.

She was at our table now, standing next to me.

"Here's your wallet," she said to me, holding my wallet in front of me. "It was on the floor."

"Oh, thank you," I said nervously, grabbing the wallet. "Thank you so much."

She smiled and patted my shoulder. "You're welcome." Then she turned around and headed back where she had come from.

And that was it.

No questions, no nothing.

I breathed a deep sigh of relief. "Wow," I said to Ollie, "that was really kind of her."

He nodded. "Yeah, that's another thing I like about this dining hall. You get to know the people who work here, and all of the staff is super nice."

I went back to eating and scarfed down the rest of the food on my plate, giving up hope that the smell or taste would bring back any memories.

After finishing our meals, Ollie and I put our dishes on the conveyor belt and then headed toward the exit.

"So where're you headed?" Ollie asked.

Good question. I knew what I had to do—find out how I got here. But how do I do that with no memory?

"Actually, I'm not sure," I said. "What about you?"

"I have to work."

"You have to work today? At the laundromat?"

"Yeah, man. I only work a few hours today, though."

An idea came to me. If I went back to the place where I had woken up the day before, I might be able to find a portal or some clue on how to get home. I didn't want to keep mooching off Ollie, but I had one more favor to ask of him.

"Can I come with you?" I asked.

He looked surprised. "Yeah, sure, man. You might get kinda bored, though, hanging out in a laundromat all afternoon."

"Actually, I have a lead that I think might get me some answers. I want to go back to the place where I first woke up yesterday."

"Gotcha. Yeah, man, that's fine. All right, let's go. My parking garage is just down the street. It's not too far from here."

"Sweet, thanks."

I followed Ollie out the door to the building. It was cloudy and colder than the day before. A beam of light escaped the gray clouds as we crossed the street, painting a pretty good picture of the way I felt. Gloomy, but hopeful. *This won't last forever*, I thought. The only thing that mattered right now was finding a way back.

Ollie had parked on the second level. When we got to his car, he smiled. "I know," he said. "It's a pretty sweet ride." He drove a beat-up red Honda Civic. It looked old to me, but maybe in this time period, it was actually new—though the faded paint and discolored door handle suggested otherwise.

I opened the door and took a seat on the stained upholstery. Ollie started the engine and pulled out of the tight parking space.

"Sorry about lunch, man," he said. "I really thought that was gonna work."

"It's all right."

As we left the parking garage, Ollie suddenly got all excited. "Oh, what about music?"

"Huh?"

"You know, songs? Music? There've been plenty of times I've listened to a certain song, and it just, like, takes me back, you know? Maybe we just need to find the right song." He shook his head. "I don't know why I didn't think of that before. Okay, let's give it a shot."

He turned on the radio. A guy started singing through the dusty speakers in Ollie's car.

I'm going to the place where love…

"Oh, this is a good one," Ollie said. "You know this one?" He cranked the volume up.

I listened intently. The lyrics expressed a desire to return home, where he's loved and feels like he belongs.

Home, I thought. *I just want to go home.*

"This one ringing any bells?" Ollie asked.

I shook my head.

"Okay, maybe this just isn't the right song." He changed the station. "Oh, this is another goodie."

I listened as another male singer's voice came through the speakers.

Stop and stare,

You start to wonder why you're here, not there…

I feel you, dude. I seriously doubted that the writer of the song had been writing about time travel (though who knows?), but I could still somehow relate the lyrics to my own situation. I guess that's the beauty of music. Regardless of a song's original meaning, everyone interprets the lyrics differently, because they relate to them in their own individual way. I wondered how much of a role music plays in my life, what type of music I listen to. The song on the radio sounded pretty dope, if you ask me.

Ollie started singing along to the music. He actually had a pretty good singing voice, which I guess made sense, since he was into theater. He looked over at me as he was jamming out and said, "Feel free to join in."

"I don't know the words."

He gave me a once-over. "You know, I wouldn't be surprised if you can sing. You kind of look like you could be the lead singer of a band, with the edgy haircut and all."

I didn't know what to make of that. I didn't think my hairstyle was "edgy," but I had also come from the future, so maybe my haircut wasn't in style yet.

After the song ended, Ollie kept changing the station, trying to find something I would recognize. He browsed through all kinds of stations: rock, pop, eighties—even a Spanish station. Some of the songs sounded vaguely familiar, but I couldn't pinpoint the source.

When we got to the laundromat, my heart started doing a slow thud. I was almost home. I could feel my hope rising like the morning sun after a cold and dark night. But if I was correct, and I found some sort of portal to take me home, then I would probably never see Ollie again. So I decided to say something to him after stepping out.

"Hey, uh, wait up, man," I called out to Ollie as he walked toward the entrance.

He stopped and looked back at me. "Yeah?"

I looked down at the ground. "I just…I wanted to say, you know, um…if I find what I'm looking for, I might not come back. So, if I don't see you again…thank you for everything. I appreciate—you know, I really appreciate you helping me out and everything."

He waved me off. "Ah, it was nothing."

"Anyway, it's been…interesting."

He chuckled. "That's the understatement of the year, man."

I smiled. "And thanks for the ride, man."

"No problem. Good luck to you, and, uh, I'll see you around."

I wasn't so sure he would.

After we parted ways, I turned around and retraced my steps from the day before. As I walked, it all started coming back to me. The rain. The car almost crashing into me. The paralyzing fear in my heart. That fear still lingered, but hope was pushing its way in. *I'm almost home*, I thought.

I turned and saw a familiar car up ahead—the one with the side-view mirror that I had used to look at my reflection. It was still parked in the same place. There was no traffic at the moment, so I moved from the sidewalk to the road and started running.

My heart picked up speed as I got closer, and not just because I was running. It was definitely this place.

I stopped. Okay, now what do I do? I didn't know. Maybe there was some sort of invisible portal I had to go through? I crept forward, like I was walking toward the edge of a cliff, and reached out my hand like someone feeling their way around in the dark. I half-expected my arm to start to vanish into thin air once I reached a certain point in the road. But nothing happened. I looked behind me. I had definitely crossed the point where I had woken up.

I didn't know what to do, and a scary thought occurred to me. What if I could no longer go back home? No. I was sure there was a way.

Maybe the portal was a one-way door, and I simply had to enter from the other way? I started to walk back toward the spot. Then I walked more quickly. After a few steps, I broke into a run. The spot where I had found myself on the ground the day before was fast approaching. I closed my eyes, bracing myself to be transported to another dimension.

It didn't happen. When I opened my eyes, I was still in the same place. Desperation creeping in, I started to run the other way again. Any residents in the neighborhood looking out their window probably thought I was a madman. Maybe I was. When I got close to the spot, I actually leapt into the air like a dog jumping through a hoop, thinking maybe the portal was floating in midair and I would be hurled into the future. But when my feet hit the ground, so did my spirits. It slowly started to sink in.

I was trapped here.

CHAPTER 6

So now what? I didn't know. I didn't want to go back to Ollie after already saying goodbye to him and keep sponging off his generosity. I had to find my own way. But I didn't know how to get by on my own.

My thoughts were interrupted by a car passing by. I got out of the way and just stood there like a dope. When the car drove off, I went back to thinking. I tried to review what I had learned so far in my mind. My name, I had learned, was Charlie Benson. I was born on November 29, 2012—a little more than four years from now. I live on 4674 Ashworth Drive—which didn't even exist yet—in Barkley, Indiana. I'm a student at Barkley University, and…that's about it.

That last piece of information seemed like the only real clue I had about my future. I thought back to earlier. Ollie's dorm was kind of on the edge of campus. I still hadn't really seen most of the campus. I wanted to go back there. But how do I get there? Wait for Ollie to finish his shift and then go back with him? That seemed logical, but I didn't want to wait for him, or keep using him for transportation. Plus, I wanted to experience the campus on my own a little. But what other option did I have? Walk there?

As if on cue, I heard a low rumble in the direction I had come from.

Like the sound of a bus driving by.

I started running toward the sound, heading back toward the laundromat. But by the time the bus came into view, it was already driving away. Without thinking, I broke into a sprint. When I finally caught up to the bus, I pounded the side of the vehicle with my hand.

"Hey! Stop the bus!"

A lady sitting on the bus saw me through the window and looked startled.

"Tell him to stop!" I shouted, still running. "Please!"

She must have said something to the driver, because the bus finally squealed to a stop.

When the doors whooshed open, I hopped on. The bus driver was the same one as the day before.

"Thank you," I said to him—sweaty, out of breath, and disheveled. "I'm sorry I'm late."

He nodded. "It's all right."

I looked at the machine in front of me. Shoot, I forgot I had to pay to use the bus. The fare, I remembered, cost a dollar twenty-five. That might not seem like a lot of money, but when you only have less than eight dollars in your wallet, well, you don't have to be an accountant to see that was a decent chunk of my remaining balance.

I started regretting my decision to chase after the bus, but I had already made a huge scene in getting the driver to stop for me. I couldn't just walk away now. So, reluctantly, I paid the fare using the change in my wallet, then took a seat.

At first, I thought about getting off at the same stop as last time, but then I realized I could probably get off closer to the campus. So when I started seeing lampposts adorned with navy-blue banners featuring Barkley's B logo, I got off at the next stop, in front of a large brick-and-concrete building. There were three students on the bus who also got off—all wearing backpacks and Barkley attire—so I followed them down a wide walkway alongside the building on the right.

I walked past a small parking lot, as well as a few benches and bike racks. Then I came across a large open area with trees and tables. A few more lampposts with the same Barkley logo were lined evenly across the plaza. I strolled past small sections of trees and bushes encircled by concrete benches. These trees were mostly bare, their leaves dispersed across the ground and crunching under my feet. Several students were sitting on the edge of a large fountain in front of a wide building that seemed to be some kind of hub for students. A few other students were tossing a frisbee back and forth on a large grassy field on the other side of the fountain. This area seemed to be the heart of campus.

I wondered how much this campus changes over the years, if it looked any different from my time as a student in the future. The fact that I still couldn't recognize any-thing—like, literally *anything*—was unnerving, to say the least.

With the fall semester in full swing, the plaza was bustling with chatty students hanging out in groups or strolling side by side. Even though I was around the same age as these students, I still felt a bit out of place since I was pretty much the only one without a backpack slung over my shoulders. That, and the fact that everything around me felt completely foreign. It was weird. This was my hometown, my university, and yet it didn't feel anything like those things. I longed to be back home—my real home in the future—and to see my family. But I had no idea how to get back, or if I even had a family. My heart sank at the thought.

I weaved through the crowd toward the wide build-ing. A couple of banners reading GO BULLDOGS hung between the brick pillars on both sides of the entrance. I climbed up the concrete steps and walked through the revolving door. There was a staircase inside that seemed to go down to some kind of bookstore, as well as two sets of curved white staircases both going up to what looked like the main floor. I walked up the staircase closest to me on the right.

The air smelled like a mix of steamed rice, soy sauce, cinnamon rolls, and pizza as I entered the food court. I let my eyes wander across the scattered tables and service counters. The place was packed with students eating and chatting.

And that was when I heard the faint sound of piano music floating through the air. The melody sounded familiar. At first, I thought it was just in my head. But then I listened again and thought, no. Somebody was definitely playing a piano in the building. Like an insect drawn to a flower, I began to follow the sound of the music. *That song*, I thought. *I've heard it before*. But where? Was it one of the songs Ollie had played on the radio? No. This one was different. But it was definitely familiar.

I walked past the food court and headed into a lounge area. I looked around the room. And there, sitting hunched over the keys of a dark-stained grand piano maybe twenty yards away, was a young woman with long and wavy brown hair. She was thin and wore a cardigan sweater over a button-down shirt, with a shiny necklace. She somehow looked familiar to me.

Something in her face…

I moved a little closer and just stood there, mesmerized as music poured from the piano. Her fingers danced across the keys. Each note hung in the air like an ethereal cloud drifting across the horizon. As she played, she rocked back and forth and swayed with the music. At one point, when she started playing higher notes on the piano, her elbows flared out and dangled in the air like a marionette.

I didn't understand why all the other students just walked by without stopping or paying attention. How could they ignore such beautiful playing? There were several students sitting in booths, either chatting or studying. Some had headphones on or earbuds in, actively tuning out the music. I seemed to be the only one truly listening. To them, it was probably just background music. But to me, it was something more. It reminded me of...home. But I didn't know why.

As soon as the song ended, I approached tentatively. When I got close enough, I gave a little wave and said, "Hey."

She looked up at me with curious blue eyes. "Oh, hey."

"That was really beautiful."

She smiled bashfully. "Thanks."

"That song...what song was that?"

Her answer surprised me. "It's just something I wrote."

My eyes widened. "You wrote that song?"

"Yeah."

But wait. If she wrote that song, then why did it sound

so familiar? Does that song become really popular or something in the future?

"I normally use one of the practice rooms," she went on, "but they were all full today. I'm a music major."

"So…you really wrote that song?" I asked again, my mind still trying to take it all in.

"Yeah."

"That's crazy. You got some serious skills."

"Thank you. Writing music is one of my favorite things to do." She tucked her hair behind her ear. "When I write, I try to channel all of my emotions into the piece I'm currently writing. Sometimes I can channel my positive energy if I had a great day, or if I'm having a bad day, I take that sadness and turn it into something beautiful. And those are usually my favorite songs."

I could feel the energy and passion bursting in her voice, like she could go on for hours. Kind of reminded me of Ollie talking about acting in his dorm room.

"That's so sick," I said. "I love that. So, what's your process like?"

"It changes with each song. Sometimes I start with a chord progression that I really like and add a melody to it, and other times, I have a melody stuck in my head—like I'll be studying or doing laundry—and then I'll have this melody that just randomly pops into my head, and then I run to the piano and find chords to go along with it." She looked at me. "Do you play?"

I hesitated. Then I said, "Uh…I don't remember."

She looked confused for a second—like, how could I not know if I played the piano?—but she didn't press the issue. "Well, you have major chords and minor chords," she explained, going into teaching mode. "Major chords sound happy." She pressed down three white keys on the piano with her left hand, producing a bright and joyful sound. "Minor chords feel a little sad and melancholic." She pressed down three different keys, creating a dark and moody sound. "Major and minor chords work together to make a beautiful song." She paused. "Life is like that, too. You need the sunshine and the rain."

Wait. Where have I heard that before?

She suddenly looked at her watch. "I have to go. Chemistry lab." She slipped on her backpack, which had been propped up against the bench, and started to leave. "Bye."

And just like that, she was gone.

After a few moments, I sat down at the piano. The seat was still warm. I stared at the keys and thought about the question the girl—I just realized I didn't get her name—had just asked me.

Did I play the piano?

For some reason, I hovered my left hand over one of the white keys without playing it. *A,* I thought. *This note is an A.* See, every note in a musical scale has a letter value—A, B, C, D, F, or G. But how did I know that?

I gently pressed down on the key. I held the note for a moment, then played two more notes with my right hand: E, followed by the next A up. Again, I wasn't sure how I knew what those notes were. I played those same three notes in succession several more times. And then I slowly started to incorporate other notes, playing new parts that were similar but contained small differences. The melody was gentle and calming, like the breaking of dawn—reminding me of some memory that was just out of reach.

As I continued, I stopped thinking about the notes and just played. And then I realized something.

I've played this song before.

I was sure of it. I wasn't making this song up on the spot. My fingers remembered this piece. Of course, my fingers didn't actually remember anything at all. But the information must have been stored somewhere in my brain. My hands knew where to go, which notes to play—without me consciously thinking about it.

The answer to the girl's question was clear now. I *did* play the piano. But several new questions emerged. When did I learn how to play? Who taught me? What song was I even playing? For now, I ignored those questions and just kept playing, getting lost in the music.

Everything around me was a blur. The place was bustling. People coming and going, enjoying their food, studying or socializing or whatever it is people did in this building. But for me, they were gone now. The room was just this piano and me. Like two old friends reconnecting.

As I played the final notes, an image flashed in my head—like a tiny flame had ignited in the darkness of my mind, illuminating a faint picture. A caring woman sitting next to me. A sheet of music in front of me. But it was like the image got caught in the flame and was already fading, with blobs of black and gray filling the spaces where details should be. I tried to grasp the memory, hold on to it, complete the obscure picture by drawing in the missing details.

And then it hit me—like a bolt of lightning that had been searching for me.

I stopped playing and gazed in the direction where the girl had disappeared. "Mom?" I whispered, as if my voice could somehow reach her.

CHAPTER 7

For a moment, I considered the possibility that my mind was playing tricks on me. Could I just be concocting wild theories—pulling images out of thin air—to help deal with my sad feels? Could I be longing to see my parents so much that I mistook my mom for a total stranger?

No.

I wasn't tripping out. It was her. There was no doubt in my mind.

A sense of hope renewed in my heart. *Mom*, I thought. I wanted to run after her and find her, tell her about everything going on. But what would I say? *I know this is hard to believe, but, you see...you gave birth to me. Well, not yet, technically. But in a few years, you will. Yep, that's right. I'm your son from the future. The boy you see before your eyes is your very own off-spring...*

Yeah, right. Who'd buy that? No, that wasn't the answer.

I glanced around the room. It was just me and my thoughts in a crowded place. I could feel the loneliness starting to creep back in, like a hunter lurking in the shadows of my heart, taking aim just when I thought I had made it out of the woods.

I'm totally alone.

No, I told myself. *I'm not alone.* I had found Mom. I might not be a glass-half-full kind of guy like Ollie, but I didn't have to act like my glass had gotten knocked over. I could at least acknowledge that finding Mom was a good thing—whether she could help me or not. But it also raised a few questions. One, what about Dad? Was he here, too? Were Mom and Dad together yet? I only had one solid memory so far. Everything else was still a blur. It was hard to keep my breathing steady as the next question tore my heart…

How do I get back home?

I didn't know. But I couldn't sit around and mope forever. I had to keep going. I had to keep trying. One memory had already resurfaced. More were bound to pop up eventually, I figured. I didn't know how I'd be okay, but I'd find a way.

There's that positive can-do attitude I thought I'd lost. I wondered how long it would last. Probably not very long. But I figured I'd ride the wave—might as well see where it led me.

I spent a few moments taking stock of my situation. If

I was going to stay here, I needed to get a job and start making money. I wouldn't survive very long with the little cash left in my wallet.

I stood up and wandered back to the food court. The lines at a hamburger place and a pizza place both snaked around for approximately a mile, so I headed toward a counter that sold submarine sandwiches and wraps, where only a few people were waiting in line.

When it was my turn in line, I stepped forward. The girl behind the counter had blonde hair under her black baseball cap and wore a green apron over a black T-shirt.

"Hi, what can I get for you?" she asked while adjusting the plastic disposable gloves on her hands.

"Are you guys hiring?" I asked, sort of quietly. I didn't care if anybody knew I was trying to get a job, but at the same time, I didn't want to draw attention to myself.

She looked up at me. "Uh, let me check. One sec." She turned toward a gruff-looking woman standing at the cash register on the opposite end of the counter. "Hey, Carla, are we hiring?"

Carla hobbled over. "You looking for a job?" she said loudly, her voice hoarse.

I nodded. "Yeah."

She reached under the counter and pulled out a pen and a piece of paper—what I assumed was a job application.

"Here," she said, slapping the pen and application

down on the counter. "Fill this out and bring it back up here when you're done."

"Thanks."

I sat down and started filling out the application, trying to block out the heavenly aroma of garlic and melted cheese coming from the pizza place nearby, which was making me hungry again already. I was tempted to buy a slice, but then I thought about the quickly-dwindling cash in my pocket and decided not to.

Yep, I needed a job pronto.

I cruised through the first few fields on the form, filling out my first and last name like a boss. But when I came across some of the other fields, I started to waver and suddenly felt like a student who forgot to study for an exam. Address? Phone number? Date of birth? Social Security number? Educational background? Employment history? What was I supposed to put for any of those?

I could hear my positive attitude go *splat* after tossing it out the window.

Yeah...I'm screwed.

I was still hovering my pen over the application, trying to magically summon a solution to my predicament, when I heard someone behind me say, "Charlie!"

I turned to see Ollie power-walking toward me with a big smile on his face.

"What's up, man?" he said when he got closer.

I managed a weak smile. "Not much, man."

He put a hand on my shoulder. "You know, I thought I might never see you again with the way you were talking earlier. Are you all right?"

Not really, I wanted to say. Instead, I went with, "Yeah, I'm fine."

"What are you up to?"

"Just trying to get a job." I pointed to the application that I had only filled out my name on so far.

"You're looking for a job?"

"Yeah. Think I'm about to throw in the towel, though. I don't know what to put for, like, any of these responses, bro."

He glanced at my application. "Yeah, all the restaurants in here are chains, so they're gonna make you fill out that type of stuff." He paused. "And I gotta tell you, Charlie, your chances of getting a job at one of these places aren't very high. A lot of people are trying to work anywhere they can these days, so competition is crazy."

Man, if even Ollie—Captain Optimism—didn't like my chances of getting a job, I must *really* be screwed.

Ollie rubbed his chin. "If you need a job, I might be able to help."

"Really?"

"Yeah, I work at this little mom-and-pop Italian restaurant downtown called DiVincenzo's, and I bet I could get you a job there. It's been a little slower than usual lately, but nothing too bad. They only hire referrals, and I know they're still looking for dishwashers. It's tough at times, but it's an honest gig. Plus, the pay is pretty good." He put a hand to his chest. "I'm a waiter, so I don't spend a lot of time in the kitchen, but maybe you'll even learn what the secret to some of that cheesy deliciousness is so you can take it back to your own kitchen."

"I thought you worked at the laundromat, though?"

"I do."

"So you have two jobs?"

"Yeah, man. Times are tough, you know? I do what I gotta do. I'm actually lucky to have two jobs. Like I said, the restaurant gig pays pretty good, especially with tips, but I also like the laundromat job because there's a lot more downtime so I can study a script or do homework while still getting paid. It's a pretty sweet gig, actually. I don't think they're hiring, though." He paused. "So, what do you say?"

I thought about it for, like, maybe two seconds. What choice did I have? I needed the money to survive.

"Okay," I said.

He smiled. "All right, let's go."

"What, you mean right now?"

"Yeah. I can take you there. It's just a short walk."

I crumpled my application and dumped it into a trash can, then set the pen on the counter and followed Ollie through the building. As we passed the lounge area, I glanced over at the unoccupied piano and felt a funny longing. I wondered what Mom was doing at this very moment, but then I remembered her saying that she had a chemistry lab.

Ollie led me to a set of doors on the opposite side of the building that opened onto a street. The sky was starting to clear up. I looked around and suddenly realized that I had just been in the same building that the bus had stopped in front of earlier. It was so big that I had thought the other side was a whole separate building.

"So, how was work?" I asked after crossing the street.

Ollie frowned. "Work was, uh, I don't want to talk about it. But anyway, what's up with you? How you doing?" Before I could answer, he added, "Oh, shoot. Your lead you were telling me about earlier. How'd that go?"

I remembered telling him about a "lead" I had that I thought would get me some answers, which had basically been my cryptic way of saying I wanted to check out the road I had woken up on to see if I could find a portal or something that would take me home.

"It went nowhere," I said, burying my hands in my pockets.

"I'm sorry, man. It's only been a day, though. It'll just take time to figure things out. Did anything interesting happen while I was at work?"

"What do you mean?"

"Like, did you remember anything?"

Should I tell him about seeing my mom? I wasn't sure, so I decided to keep it vague. "Thought I saw someone I recognized."

"Really? Who was it?"

Once again, I didn't want to lie—but I wasn't up for telling the full truth either. I didn't even know this guy until yesterday. So, again, I kept it vague. "Somebody important to me."

"Did you talk to them?"

"Yeah."

"And?"

"They didn't know who I was."

"That's so weird."

"Yeah," I said, even though it made perfect sense to me. At least, the logic of it made sense. Obviously, Mom didn't recognize me because I hadn't been born yet. But if I hadn't been born yet, then how the heck could I even be here in the first place? That still made zero sense. I mean, how did I get here? I tried to sort through it, but nothing came to me. I could feel a gnawing fear growing in my stomach that I might be trapped here forever.

"Maybe they just reminded you of someone you know," Ollie suggested. "You know, like, I was walking back to my dorm late at night one time, and this car drove by, and some dude in the backseat popped his head out the window and shouted, 'Hey, Kevin!' at me, thinking I was him."

I had already considered that possibility—that I had confused my mom with a random stranger as some kind of weird coping mechanism—but there was no way. I can't really explain it—I just knew. Like, she's my mom, you know?

"He was definitely hammered, though," Ollie added.

"Yeah, I don't really think that's what happened to me."

He shook his head. "This whole thing is weird."

"Yeah."

We walked past a hamburger chain, then crossed another street and passed various shops, including a running store, a burrito place, and a smoothie shop that I recognized from the green punch card in my wallet. There was a lot of construction going on in the area, with a bunch of orange signs, cones, and barricades scattered throughout the sidewalks and streets.

DiVincenzo's was located in an old brick building. When we arrived, we walked under the tattered dark green awning out front before stepping inside.

My first thought when entering the restaurant: *whoa.* I felt like I had suddenly been transported to Venice or Rome. The best word I can think of to describe the place was *artsy.* Colorful murals adorned the walls. The spacious high ceiling was painted in bright blue with streaks of white to resemble a clear daytime sky with a few thin clouds. The patio-style seating area was surrounded by

Renaissance-style columns, with a small fountain sitting in the middle.

The aroma reminded me of the pizza place back at the previous building, only somehow even more enticing. I could smell the pizza dough, garlic, tomato sauce, and other ingredients bubbling in the oven. It wasn't even five o'clock yet, and the place was hopping. If business really was slower than usual, I wondered how crowded this restaurant would normally be. I also wondered if this place still exists in the future—is still this popular—or if this was simply its heyday before later getting shut down.

"Hey, Ollie," the guy at the service counter—a young man wearing a branded raglan shirt—said. He and Ollie pounded fists. Ollie seemed to be friends with everyone around here.

"Hey, Frankie. Is Tony in?"

"Yeah, he's in the back. You want me to go get him?"

"That'd be awesome, thanks." Ollie gestured to me. "This is my buddy Charlie. He's applying for a job."

I stuck out my hand. "Hi, nice to meet you."

He smiled and shook my hand. "Nice to meet you, too. I'm Frankie." After letting go of my hand, he said, "I'll be right back," and disappeared into the kitchen.

A few moments later, he reemerged with a burly bald dude behind him. He was built like a wild boar. Stocky and muscular, with a large head and short, thick neck. He wore a crimson-red polo with sleeves stretching all the way down to his elbows. He looked like he could have been a professional MMA fighter or linebacker. Not the kind of guy you want to mess with. He seemed friendly enough, though, I guess.

"Heyyy, Ollie," he said with a New York accent. "I appreciate you stopping by."

Ollie smiled and shook his hand. "Hey, Tony, good to see you."

Tony turned to me. "So, you looking for a job?"

"Yes, sir."

"What's your name?"

"Uh, Charlie," I said, reaching out my hand. When he shook my hand, I thought he was going to break it.

"I haven't seen you around," he said. "You new to the area?"

"Uh, yeah, something like that."

"Do you live nearby? Because we're very particular about punctuality."

Not sure what to say, I went with, "Uh, yeah, I'm staying in the area."

"We're looking for dishwashers right now. Is that position okay with you?"

"Yes, sir."

"Good. I should warn you, though, it's not easy. You'll learn what hard work is right off the bat. It's hot, sweaty work and takes time to get into the rhythm of it and learn how to be efficient. You still interested?"

"Yes, sir."

"Pay is ten dollars an hour."

I didn't know whether that was a little or a lot. I didn't care. It was something.

"Okay," I said with a nod.

He folded his arms. "Look, you seem like a good kid, so I'll give you a shot."

I smiled, relieved. "Thank you, sir."

"When can you start?"

"Uh…now?"

He chuckled. "That's what I like to hear. But let's wait a day. You'll start ten o'clock tomorrow morning. Sound good?"

"Yes, sir."

"Okay. Thanks for coming."

As we walked out of the restaurant, Ollie high-fived me. "See? What I'd tell you, man?"

I smiled. It's funny how even in the most challenging moments, you can have moments when you let yourself forget for a few seconds.

"Thank you, man."

We headed back down the sidewalk.

"Oh, I almost forgot," Ollie said, "I was gonna show you the store where you can buy sheets and a pillow for your bed. You wanna go there now? I have a little bit of time before I have to get back to campus. Oh, I just thought of this. You're probably gonna need some more clothes, too. I can let you borrow some of mine, but we can also get some from the store, too."

And there it was—that familiar sinking feeling yet again. Sure, I'd just secured a job, but the job wouldn't pay me right away. I barely had any money left. Ollie had already done so much for me. I couldn't just keep taking and taking.

"No, man," I said, "that's okay."

"What, man? It's no problem."

I shook my head. "No, I've been thinking, and, uh…you know, I think I'm holding you up."

"Ah, no, don't say that about yourself. That's not true, Charlie. That really isn't true. Come on, let's go," he urged me. "I'll drive you there."

"No, I have no money."

"That's okay. If you want, I could loan you the money to buy the stuff you need."

"That's really great of you, but I couldn't."

"It's all right. You can pay me back later."

"Look, Ollie, I appreciate what you're trying to do here, especially since you're the only one who knows what I'm going through…"

Well, sort of, I thought.

"But…" I went on, trying to find the right way to put this, "I can't keep doing this to you. It just wouldn't be right."

"Doing what to me?"

"You know…freeloading off you."

Ollie made a face. "Freeloading? Dude, it's a loan. I already said you can pay me back later."

"But what about your dorm? Shouldn't I be paying you rent or something?"

He shook his head. "It's okay. You're going through a lot, man. Don't tell yourself you can't lean on someone else, 'cause we all need to sometimes. And if housing becomes an issue, we can figure something out." He started walking away. "All right, let's do it."

I took a deep breath and called out to him. "Why are you helping me, Ollie?"

But I didn't get an answer. He didn't turn around or say anything. He just kept walking. I gave up interrogating him and walked alongside him.

Honestly, I don't know what I would have done without him.

A few minutes later, I was back in Ollie's car. He played a pop station and sang along again.

As we drove by a hospital, I tensed up. "Wait," I said. "Are you taking me to the hospital?"

"Nah, man, it just happens to be on the way. I mean, the offer is still on the table, but I won't take you there against your will."

I leaned back against the headrest for a second, relieved.

"That gives me an idea, though," Ollie said.

I didn't like where this was going.

"There's this scene in *The Outsiders* where Dallas is driving Ponyboy to the hospital to see Johnny."

Ponyboy? I thought. *What kind of a name is that?*

He went on. "It happens a little differently in the play, you know, due to logistical reasons or whatever, but it's in both the book and the movie, toward the end. I've been racking my brain for the longest time trying to figure out how I want to approach the last few scenes. Like, what do I want to put in your face right here, and what do I want you to infer, you know? I think a lot of acting is not only what you do, but what you don't do, and the things that you're thinking. I feel like I've been trying to solve this unsolvable riddle. Anyway, maybe we could reenact it, you know?" His face started beaming. "This is perfect. I'll be Dallas, obviously, and you'll be Ponyboy. You think you can act like Ponyboy?"

I puffed out a snort. "I don't even know how to act like myself."

He laughed. "That's the greatest challenge of all, my friend. Always be yourself, not the person you pretend to be." He turned his head and smiled at me. "Unless you're an actor, of course."

"That's not really what I meant, man. I mean, I don't even know who the heck Ponyboy is."

"Hey, that's okay. You don't even gotta say anything, man. This takes place right after a fight scene, so all you gotta do is pretend you just got knocked around by a bunch of dudes in a gang. That shouldn't be too hard, given the way you looked yesterday."

True, I thought. I flashed back to the day before. Waking up. Blood streaming down my face. My head throbbing. My stomach turning. I started feeling sick all over again just thinking about it.

"I don't feel so good, man," I said, leaning back against the headrest again.

"Hey, that's perfect, man. All right, let's do this." He turned the radio down and took a deep breath.

"I was crazy," he said in an exasperated voice, suddenly putting on a New York accent like Tony and breaking into character. "You know that, kid? I was crazy about wanting Johnny to stay out of trouble, man." He started to raise his voice. "If he was smart like me, he wouldn't have been in this mess. If he was smart like me, he wouldn't have ran in that church, man." He paused and looked at me. "You better wise up, Pony, man. You just better wise up, man. You get tough like me, and you don't get hurt." He paused again. "Watch out for yourself," he said, his voice starting to break, as if on the verge of tears, "and nothing"—he smacked the car's infotainment system, startling me and nearly breaking it, not to mention his hand—"nothing can touch you, man."

There were a few seconds of silence as Ollie choked back what I couldn't tell whether were real or fake tears.

"You good, bro?" I asked.

His face broke into a smile. "Yeah," he said, slipping back into his normal self. "That felt good, man. That helped a lot. I think I'm starting to get it now. Thank you, bro."

"Yeah," I said, even though I hadn't really done anything.

Say what you will about Ollie, but you couldn't question his commitment. The dude was the definition of dedication. Most people would probably just wing this part, but he was giving it so much thought. And he was always carrying around and studying the script.

He turned the radio back up and went into concert mode again.

I closed my eyes, the sun beaming down on me through the windshield. The song on the radio ended, and another one began.

CHAPTER 8

I got to DiVincenzo's fifteen minutes before my shift was scheduled to start the next day. I wasn't sure if I would remember how to get there, and the last thing I wanted to do was show up late on my first day, so I played it safe. But fifteen minutes almost seemed a little *too* early, so I waited outside for ten minutes—leaning against the brick wall, watching cars and people go by—before finally stepping inside.

Once again, a wave of wonderful cheesy aromas hit my senses. Frankie greeted me at the counter and showed me to the kitchen, where I met the rest of my coworkers. The kitchen was surprisingly clean. I don't know why, but I had expected something filthy and grimy for some reason.

They had me working with another guy who showed me the ropes and offered tips to help keep me as dry and clean as possible. I asked a lot of questions and tried to learn how to do things more efficiently. I figured if I was more efficient, I'd expend less effort than wasting energy stressing and complaining.

I'd asked Ollie a few questions and tried to do a little research beforehand and found out that dishwashing often has a high turnover rate. So I was pretty nervous going in and kind of expected the worst. Everything stacked in bizarre and dangerous piles. People berating me and constantly pestering me for specific dishes. Stuff like that. But thankfully, I didn't experience any of that. I had to rewash one of the pans that got sent back to me early on, but the cook was nice enough about it, and I learned my lesson. I felt a little embarrassed, but I guess making mistakes is how you learn and grow.

Tony told me I would get a thirty-minute break every shift with one free meal, so during my break, I wolfed down a delicious cheese pizza before getting back to the grind. For the whole afternoon, I didn't think about how I was stuck in the past and only thought about pots and pans and dishes and making sure they were clean. In that sense, it was a nice distraction from my predicament. Don't get me wrong. The work was still hectic, hot, and gross, but it certainly could have been a lot worse at some other places, I imagined. I was glad Ollie had gotten me a job here. Like I said before, I don't know what I would have done without him.

It was a Friday—Halloween, actually—so the place was packed. My shift ended at six, though, so I didn't have to work during some of the busiest hours. Tony probably didn't want me to get too overwhelmed on my first day and be tempted to quit. My shift was eight hours long, which I had thought would drag on forever, but the hours flew by.

When my shift ended, I hung my apron on the little hook and headed back to Reinhart. The sky was starting to turn dark as I made the walk.

When I stepped into Ollie's dorm room, I glanced at Ollie, then did a double take. He was draped in a long black robe, and underneath he wore a gray V-neck sweater over a white shirt and red-and-gold striped tie. He was also wearing round glasses and waving around some kind of stick or…wand?

"What's with the getup?" I asked.

"It's not a getup. It's a uniform," he said, with a tinge of annoyance in his voice. He shook his head. "Muggle."

"Muggle?" I said, confused.

"Non-magic folk."

"Oh," I said, even more confused. I plopped down in one of the beanbag chairs. "So, what's with the uniform, then?"

"It's a school uniform."

"Barkley requires students to wear uniforms?"

"No."

"Then what's the uniform for?"

"Hogwarts, of course," he said, adjusting his robe.

I thought for a moment. Then it finally clicked. "You mean…from *Harry Potter*?"

He smiled. "Ah, you're finally starting to catch on, my friend. There may be hope for you yet." He paused. "I'm going to a Halloween party tonight with my girlfriend. She should be coming over in a few minutes."

"She's coming here?"

"Yeah, hope you don't mind."

"No, that's fine." I was actually looking forward to finally meeting her.

"You wanna come with us?"

"Nah, I'm good. I'm really tired."

When Ollie turned around, I suddenly noticed a bright red cut on his forehead in the shape of a lightning bolt.

"Yo, what happened to your face, dude?" I asked, concerned.

"What? Oh, that," he said, rubbing his forehead. "It's just a scar."

"How'd you get it?" I asked, wondering why I hadn't noticed it before.

"Failed murder attempt," he said calmly.

What…?

Noticing the color that was probably draining from my face, Ollie smiled and said, "Relax, dude. It's just part of the backstory for the character I'm dressed as."

"Oh…okay."

Ollie closed the door and looked in the mirror hanging

on the back of the door as he straightened his tie. "So, how was your first day at the new job?"

It took a few seconds for me to gather my thoughts and form a reply. "Pretty crazy, but all right, I guess," I finally said.

"First days are always the hardest. My first day, I spilled Coke all over this girl and probably ruined her dress. I felt so bad. Had to get another waiter to take over my table since I was so embarrassed."

I felt a little better now about having a pan sent back to me. That didn't sound nearly as embarrassing as Ollie's story.

After fixing his tie, Ollie moved closer to the mirror and gazed longingly at it. "Mum?" he whispered in a British accent. He turned his head slightly to the right. "Dad?" He gently pressed his hand against the mirror.

"Uh...you good, bro?" I asked, thinking maybe he really had injured his head.

He snapped out of his trance, or...whatever that was. "I was just looking into the Mirror of Erised," he explained.

"The what?"

"The Mirror of Erised," he said again. "It's a magical mirror that shows people their deepest desire. The name *Erised* is actually *desire* spelled backward—you know, as if reflected in a mirror."

"Oh, cool." Another *Harry Potter* reference, I figured.

"Obviously, it's not really the Mirror of Erised. It's just pretend."

I nodded. "So, when's your girlfriend coming again?" I asked, starting to wonder if she was pretend, too.

"She'll be here."

There was a knock on the door.

"She's here!"

I stood up as Ollie opened the door. And there, standing in the doorway, with the same long and wavy brown hair and blue eyes, was the girl I'd seen playing the piano the other day.

Mom.

CHAPTER 9

I stood there, stunned.

She wore basically the same getup—er, uniform—as Ollie. Same black robe, white shirt, red-and-gold tie, and gray sweater. Only she wore a skirt, while Ollie wore pants.

"Hermione!" Ollie said, cheesing real hard. He had pronounced her name as *Her-my-oh-nee*.

She smiled and stepped into the room.

"This is my new roommate, Charlie," Ollie said, gesturing toward me.

Seeing her as Mom for the first time made me want to hug her, but I knew that'd be weird for her—and Ollie—so instead I stuck out my hand and said, "Hi, nice to meet you."

A flash of recognition crossed her face when she shook my hand. "Do I know you?"

I'm your son.

Obviously, I couldn't actually say that. Ollie, for one,

would have a few questions. And…yeah, I already went over this. No one would believe me if I told them I was from the future.

"Oh, wait," she continued, "I talked to you the other day at the union when I was playing the piano, right?"

The union? So I guess that's what that building was called.

I nodded. "Yeah."

"You two know each other?" Ollie said. "That's wild."

You have no idea, man, I thought.

"I'm Rachel, by the way."

I looked at her, confused. "I thought your name was Hermione?"

She laughed. "No, that's just the character I'm dressed as for Halloween. My real name is Rachel Murphy."

Rachel Murphy? So Murphy must be my mom's maiden name, I figured. Then another thought occurred to me. Or maybe it had been on my mind since I first saw her in the doorway and I was just now processing it.

Wait. If Mom and Ollie were dating, could Ollie possibly be…my dad? And if so, why didn't I remember him?

Ollie rested his arm on her shoulder. "You know, I didn't find out until, like, the fourth book in the series that I had been pronouncing Hermione's name wrong in my head the entire time. I always pronounced it as *Her-mer-oyn* for some reason."

Mom/Rachel made a face and stifled a laugh. "Ew, gross. That sounds a lot like *hemorrhoid*."

Ollie burst out laughing. "It does, doesn't it?"

"That doesn't even make sense. How would you get *Her-mer-oyn* out of that?"

He made a production of gesturing toward her. "Spoken like Hemorrhoid herself."

"Don't call me that."

"Fine. I'll call you Rhoid for short."

She made a face again. "That just makes me think of steroids. You know, like, roid rage?"

"That's better than thinking of hemorrhoids."

Man, this was some first interaction to witness between my potential parents.

Hemorrhoid—I mean, Hermione—I mean, Rachel—rolled her eyes. "Whatever."

Ollie lifted his arm, letting his robe slide down his wrist so he could look at his watch. "Well, we should probably get going." He looked at me. "You sure you don't want to come?"

Now I really did sort of want to come—I mean, now that I knew Mom would be there. Maybe being around her would evoke more memories. But I was exhausted from working all day and sweaty and gross. I didn't have a costume either. Plus, I'd be third-wheeling big-time—not that I would really care or anything.

"Yeah, I'm good," I said. "But thanks for the invite."

"All right, suit yourself." He looked at Rachel. "You ready?"

She nodded. "Yeah."

Ollie turned to me and put a hand on my shoulder. "Hold down the fort while I'm gone, okay?"

"Okay, have fun," I said, "…but not too much fun."

I don't know why I had added that last part.

Ollie smiled at me. "No promises."

They started for the door when I suddenly thought of something. "Hey, Ollie…"

He stopped and turned around. "Yeah?"

I wasn't sure how to ask this, but I figured what the heck. "This is, like, a really random question, but what's your last name?"

He gave me a curious look. "Why?"

"Oh, I'm just curious, is all," I said, trying to sound nonchalant. "Like, I'm your roommate or whatever, and I don't even know your last name."

He pushed his glasses back up his nose. "It's Potter," he said in a British accent.

Rachel punched him in the arm.

"Right," he said, staying in character. "Sorry." Then, finally ditching the accent, he said, "Um…it's Jones."

Jones? But my last name was Benson. So…he's not my dad, then? If Ollie's not my dad…then who is? And what happens with Ollie and Rachel's relationship in the future?

Not sure what to say, I settled for, "Oh…cool."

Rachel smiled at me and said, "It was nice to officially meet you."

"Yeah…you, too."

Ollie waved with the hand that wasn't holding the wand and said, "Later, dude."

"Bye."

He closed the door on their way out.

I could hear Ollie casting fake spells as they walked down the hallway. Then the whole floor fell quiet. No music blasting from any of the rooms. No residents hanging around the common area. They must have all been out partying, as well, I figured.

The silence wasn't so bad until I looked in the mirror and felt a deep pang in my chest. Why did I feel so lonely after every time Mom left? Maybe I should have gone with them. I felt like a scared little boy experiencing separation anxiety. Like I had reverted to some weird state of childlike dependency.

I flashed back to my conversation with Ollie before Rachel had shown up. He had told me that this mirror—The Mirror of Erised, as he called it—would show the deepest desire of a person's heart. I knew it was all make-believe, of course. But still, as I stood in front of the mirror, I pictured my mom standing right behind my reflection, twenty-some years in the future, smiling at me. A man appeared in silhouette right next to her. The figure was dark and featureless, like a black hole had been carved into the mirror in the shape of my dad.

I reached my hand out and touched the mirror as though maybe this was actually the portal that would send me home. My fingertips started to feel cold on the glass.

For a moment, I thought I felt a hand on my shoulder, but when I looked behind me, no one was there. And I was alone once again.

CHAPTER 10

The next day was a Saturday. I was walking down the hallway on the top floor of Reinhart when I saw Ollie and Ronnie playing some kind of game in the common area.

Ollie turned around when he heard my footsteps.

"Charlie, hey. Hi," he said, smiling.

"Hey."

"I gotta go to work, man," Ronnie said, grabbing his backpack.

"Okay, see ya, man."

"See ya." He nodded at me. "'Sup, Charlie?"

"Hey, man."

Ollie pointed to Ronnie as he walked past. "MVP right there." He turned to me. "Okay, you're up, Charlie." He handed me a small squishy orange basketball. Then he backed up several feet and held out his long arms in a circle, either hugging an imaginary tree or forming a human basketball hoop.

Based on the ball in my hand, I guessed the latter.

"The game is on the line," Ollie continued, impersonating a sports announcer. "Charlie Benson, star point guard for Barkley, has the ball at the top of the key. The Bulldogs are down by two points in the final seconds. Here we go. Three, two one…"

Confused, I tossed up the ball.

"For the win!" Ollie continued.

The ball dropped through Ollie's arms and bounced off his leg.

"Bang!" Ollie shouted, raising his arms in celebration. "And the crowd goes wild!"

I started cheesing for some reason, even though I knew it was kind of silly.

"You ever been to a basketball game before?" Ollie asked, picking up the ball from the floor.

I tried to think, but nothing came to me. My smile faded. "I don't remember."

"Right. Sorry, I keep forgetting. How's that going with your memory, by the way? Any memories come back yet?"

I thought about the only memory I had recovered, of Mom—Ollie's girlfriend—giving me a piano lesson. But, obviously, I couldn't tell him about that. So I just shook my head and said, "No."

"That's rough. Sorry, man." He pulled two tickets from one of his jacket pockets and held them up. "Anyway, do you want to go to the game with me?"

"What game?"

"Barkley versus Briarwood. First home basketball game of the season. It'll be fun. Basketball runs deep in this state, and especially this school. Home games go pretty hard, I'm not gonna lie. I feel like it's something every Barkley student should experience at least once."

"You're a basketball fan?" I said, surprised.

He nodded. "Huge. I think I'm the only person in the world who loves basketball and theater equally. I'm telling you, man, basketball *is* theater. It's a performance. Everyone has a role to play. That's why I love both." He paused. "So, what do you say?"

"What about Rachel?"

He shook his head. "She can't make it. She has a family thing." He paused. "You can totally say no, Charlie. I just...you know, I already bought the tickets, and I don't want to go alone."

"Sure, Ollie."

"All right, that's, uh, cool," he said, handing me one of the tickets. "Oh, speaking of tickets, that reminds me..." He slipped out another ticket from the other pocket in his jacket and gave it to me. "Here."

"What's this?"

"A ticket to my show in a few days. You don't have to go, Charlie, but it'd mean a lot to me if you came."

I looked at the ticket. The show was at seven on Tuesday, November 4th. Just three days away.

"I'll be there," I said, assuming I'd still be in this time period then.

"Really?" he said, his face lighting up.

"Yeah, man."

"Awesome. Man, it's gonna be so much fun. I can't wait." He walked past me. "All right, let's go."

"Where are we going?"

"To the game, remember?"

"Right now?"

"Yeah, we don't got much time before tip-off."

I followed him through the hallway, down the stairs, and out the building.

It was a beautiful fall day out. Sunlight glinted through the last few leaves on the trees in our path, illuminating the auburn, yellow, and orange veins that ran through them. The campus seemed to be painted in a sea of navy blue as students and fans from every direction streamed toward Hayward Fieldhouse.

We got in line and eventually stepped through the doors. A guy with gray hair wearing a yellow EVENT STAFF shirt scanned our tickets. Banners of past Barkley greats adorned the walls. There was a dude decked out in Barkley gear sitting with his back against the wall and had a bulldog on a leash. At first, I wondered why the event staff would allow an animal in the facility, but then I realized the bulldog was probably the university's official live mascot. The dog was panting, its big pink tongue lolling out, and looking all around. I kind of wanted to stop and ask to pet the dog, but I kept walking.

We walked up a ramp, which led to an open concourse surrounding the stands. Before we headed to our seats, we made stops to use the restroom and grab some food.

We showed our tickets to the usher monitoring our section in the upper deck. After finding our seats, I glanced around at the packed arena. There didn't seem to be a bad—or empty—seat in the house. The crowd was buzzing. The pep band played something upbeat and energetic. Natural light streamed in from the huge rectangular windows on one end of the gym, aligned like a symmetric bar graph. Metal beams stretched across the rounded ceiling.

Down on the court, balls arced through the air—some swishing through the hoop and others clanging off the rim—as the two teams shot around. Barkley was in their home white jerseys with navy-blue lettering, and Briarwood was in royal blue with white lettering.

As the warm-up clock winded down, both teams headed to their respective benches. The public address announcer welcomed the spectators, and then Barkley's pep band played the national anthem. Before long, the public address announcer introduced the starting lineups, beginning with Briarwood. The crowd was quiet but respectful as each name got called out.

The lights dimmed, painting the court in a soft blue glow. Cheerleaders danced on the sideline. A guy ran across the court waving a Barkley flag.

"Bulldog nation, stand proud, rise up, get loud. It's time to reveal the starting lineup for your Barkley Bulldogs!"

The crowd erupted.

"Starting at guard, a six-two sophomore from Philadelphia, Pennsylvania, number three, Robbie Benson!"

My heart stopped. Robbie…Benson? That had to be a coincidence, right? I mean, Benson had to be a pretty common last name. There was no way he could actually be…or could he?

Robbie Benson calmly got up and high-fived his teammates around him after being introduced. He looked a lot like…me. Same curly black hair, only shorter—at least, on top.

I didn't get it. Does Mom go from dating a theater kid to…a basketball player?

I glanced over at Ollie. He seemed oblivious to the connection between our last names.

Eventually, the starters took their positions around center court, and the game was underway. Both teams got out to a hot start, sinking a lot of their early shot attempts.

As the game went on, the matchup was a back-and-forth brawl, like a heavyweight clash. It seemed like every time one team would hit a big shot, the other team would storm down the court and answer with a clutch bucket of their own.

As I watched, I realized that I must have played basketball growing up. I recognized everything happening down on the court. Fast breaks. Steals. Rebounds. Three-pointers. Fouls. Free throws. Screens to set up an open man. Even the gym felt strangely familiar. The atmosphere was crazy. The echoes, the vibrations, and the cheers all blended into a deafening roar.

My eyes stayed mostly on Robbie Benson. He played point guard and was almost like a coach on the floor. He moved the ball well, getting his teammates into position and orchestrating the offense. But the most elite part of his game was his defense. He recorded several steals and flew all over the court, taking charges, boxing out, and basically doing every little gritty thing that makes coaches swoon, and makes opposing fans foam with rage—while secretly wishing he played for their team. He constantly played at maximum speed, like he only had one gear—full throttle.

Before I knew it, it was crunch time. The crowd hushed after a Briarwood guard hit a clutch three-pointer from the corner to give his team a two-point lead with only nine seconds left. No timeouts left and the clock dwindling, Robbie Benson broke Briarwood's press with that squirrely quickness. He tossed the ball to a forward on the elbow. He handed the ball back to Robbie on the wing. Robbie dribbled toward the baseline, looking for a lane to the basket or an open teammate. Only a few seconds remaining, he crossed over to the left and picked up his dribble a few feet inside the arc, his man sticking to him like glue. Nobody open, Robbie pivoted and leapt, releasing a tough fadeaway jumper. I watched the ball sail through the air as the buzzer sounded.

The shot fell short and glanced off the front of the rim.

The crowd let out a collective groan as the Briarwood players started to celebrate. And just like that, the game was over. I glanced up at the scoreboard. The final score was 78-76, Briarwood.

The teams headed back to their locker rooms after shaking hands, and the crowd started shuffling out. Ollie and I hung around for several minutes as the gym emptied before heading out.

After walking down the ramp, Ollie joined a long line of people waiting to use the restroom that extended out the door. I leaned against the wall in the concourse area and waited. Laughter and chatter filled the space, despite the loss. But there was another sound that eventually broke through the rest.

Someone was dribbling a basketball in the gym.

The sound called out to me, kind of like the sound of Rachel playing the piano the other day. I was drawn to it. There was something comforting and inviting about the sound. It reminded me of a heartbeat, with a steady, rhythmic pulse.

Thump, thump, thump, thump.

I started walking through the tunnel toward the court. I didn't know if I was even allowed on the court, but nobody was stopping me, so I figured what the heck.

When I reached the end of the tunnel, I stopped and just stared for a few seconds. Robbie Benson was on the side of the court closest to me putting up mid-range jumpers—the same shot he'd missed at the end of the game earlier. His face was coated in sweat. He was locked in, completely focused on the drill.

My heart started racing as soon as I stepped onto the waxed hardwood, which gleamed under the lights. The empty seats towered all around me. Everything felt sacred, like I was in a sanctuary.

The court looked much bigger up close and personal, kind of like how automobiles look like toy cars from a plane window but feel much bigger when sitting in one— well, unless you're sitting in a cramped compact car like Ollie's, I guess. I didn't know how I could make that connection between planes and cars. I must have flown on a plane at some point in my life, but I couldn't remember when.

I tentatively wandered over to the baseline and moved under the basket. Robbie was about to go up for another shot but then hesitated for a second and looked at me.

I could see now that it wasn't just sweat coating his face.

It was also tears.

Without saying anything, he tossed up a shot. The ball swished through the net.

I grabbed the rebound. As soon as the ball touched my hands, a strange exhilarating feeling came over me. Like the ball had magic powers or something. The leather felt smooth and soft. I tossed the ball back to Robbie. He made a move and took another shot. I grabbed the rebound and returned the ball to him.

We kept going like that for a while. He put up shots from all around this end of the court. He made some, missed some, and it got me thinking about how shooting hoops is like a metaphor for life. And then something happened.

A new memory unlocked.

I'm probably eight or nine years old. I'm sitting on my dad's lap in his office after one of my basketball games, holding a basketball. My mom is also in the room. I can see her face. I can't see my dad's face, but it's him— Robbie. There's a desk in the middle of the room, but we're sitting on a chair in the corner, my mom in another chair right next to us. I'm feeling discouraged for some reason. The walls are painted navy blue. There's a white Barkley logo painted on one of the walls.

Wait. Is my dad a basketball coach here in the future?

Anyway, my dad is telling me something. Something about the legendary baseball player Babe Ruth breaking the record for most home runs in a season. Then he tells me—if I remember correctly—that Ruth had also struck out more than any other player in the same season.

But why would he tell me that? Maybe I had a bad game and missed a bunch of shots. Or maybe I didn't shoot at all, afraid to miss. You can't miss if you don't shoot, right? That might be true, but you also can't score any points playing that way.

I think my dad was trying to teach me something like that.

As I watched Robbie shoot, I started to realize something. He wasn't some shallow jock like I had initially suspected. He was a passionate person not afraid to chase a dream.

Sound like anyone else I knew?

Maybe Ollie and Robbie weren't all that different. Sure, their personalities might have been a little different. But their core values—courage, determination, passion— were pretty much the same. They both had it in them— that obsession and diligence to pursue a single thing over a long time.

Robbie kept shooting, and I kept rebounding for him. Neither of us said a word. We didn't have to.

I snatched another rebound and was about to pass the ball back to Robbie when I heard a voice say, "Robbie?"

It was one of the assistant coaches, standing at the edge of the tunnel.

"Coach Brady wants to see you in his office."

"Okay, Coach."

The coach disappeared into the tunnel.

Robbie looked at me. "I gotta go."

I nodded.

"Thanks for rebounding for me," he said, starting to walk toward the tunnel.

"No problem."

One of his shoes squeaked on the court as he turned toward me again. "What's your name?"

"Charlie."

He flashed a weak smile. "Cool name."

You and Mom gave it to me, I thought.

"Uh, thanks."

"I'm Robbie."

I nodded again. "Nice to meet you."

"Yeah, you, too."

"See ya."

"Bye."

As I watched him walk off the court, I couldn't help but smile. The college Dad was pretty cool. Mom was cool, too. Do I ever think that in the future? I doubted it. But seeing them at the same age as me made me realize...they're a lot more like me than I probably think growing up.

After Robbie left, I started to dribble toward the ball rack on the sideline. The sound echoed through the vast space. I wondered if Ollie was looking around for me, and then a sad thought struck me—like a hard chest pass to the gut when you're not expecting it.

If Robbie and Rachel—Dad and Mom—get married in the future…Ollie and Rachel are eventually going to have to break up.

CHAPTER 11

I worked at DiVincenzo's again the next day and stayed until closing, which was kind of a pain. Everything came back to me and the other guy washing dishes. And I mean *everything*. Like, literally every single dish. I didn't get back until almost midnight.

The room was dark when I got back. The TV was on, turned real quiet to some sports station playing the top highlights from the day. But Ollie's eyes were on the script in his hand, per usual. He was sprawled out on the bottom bunk, using his other hand to prop up his head. I didn't know how he could read in the near darkness, with the only illumination coming from the small TV screen and the moonlight pouring in.

"Hey," he said, without taking his eyes off the script.

"Hey."

I wanted to climb straight into my bunk and get some sleep, but I forced myself to take a shower since I was all stinky and sweaty. I was hoping more memories would materialize and to find some kind of clue to help me get back to my own world, but I was too tired to think about time travel or my parents or anything. After I showered, I went back to the room and just slept.

When Ollie got back from one of his classes on Monday, he asked me what my plans for lunch were.

I shrugged. "I don't really know."

"You want to have lunch with Rachel and me? We're gonna go to this sub place downstairs."

"You mean, here in the building?"

"Yeah, it's tucked away in the basement, but it's really good. I lived in this same dorm my freshman year, and I didn't even know about it until, like, finals week of my first semester when my roommate showed it to me. It's kind of like a secret hideout. Although there's always a long line when I go there, so maybe not so secret."

I rubbed my head. "Sure, I'll go with you."

"All right, let's do it."

Third-wheeling for the win.

I followed Ollie down the stairs to the first floor. We walked past the main entryway and took a spiral staircase down to what I guessed was the basement. At the bottom of the steps, Ollie turned left, and I followed him around a corner. As Ollie turned right, I glanced to my left at a dark and eerie corridor with several doors on both sides.

"What's that?" I asked, pointing toward the corridor.

Ollie looked in the direction I was pointing. "No idea. I've never really seen anyone go back there. Pretty creepy, huh?"

No kidding.

"In fact, you know that ghost story I was telling you about the other day—about the student who went missing?"

"Yeah?"

"I'm pretty sure that hallway is where she was last seen." He looked at me and said in a spooky voice, "Or so the story goes."

I swallowed and hurried away. We walked down a ramp and met up with Rachel down the corridor. She wore jeans and a black, lightweight puffer jacket. We got in line. Sure enough, the line was lengthy and stretched around the corner and into the corridor.

I shuffled forward with the line and then glanced toward the seating area. Several booths lined the wall on both sides of the small, cozy room—most of them occupied. A few more round tables and chairs were scattered across the wood floor in the middle of the room, as well as a random pool table. I also noticed a slightly elevated platform on the far end of the room, what looked like a small stage or something.

The line moved forward. The checker scanned Ollie's and Rachel's student IDs. I took out my wallet. I had finally gotten paid at my last shift at DiVincenzo's—which

I had requested to receive in cash—and, thankfully, had enough to cover the cost of the meal on my own. But in the back of my mind, I was thinking about how I still needed to pay Ollie back for the items he had helped me buy at the store the other day.

The checker handed me a small brown paper bag. I picked out a bag of chips and a piece of fruit, which I guess came with the meal, and slipped them into the paper bag.

When it was my turn in line, I ordered a cold turkey sub, which they wrapped in a red-and-white checkered paper sheet. I dropped the sub into the bag, then poured myself a drink into a disposable cup and followed Ollie and Rachel to the only empty booth on the right side of the room near the exit.

After setting my food down on the table, I went back and poured myself a cup of chicken noodle soup and grabbed a chocolate chip cookie and a few napkins before returning to the table.

"Time for a wee break," Ollie said in a Scottish accent as we were about to sit down, out of the blue.

"What?" I said.

I was still getting used to Ollie's offbeat nature.

"I have to tinkle," he said in a normal voice, which was weird because...that didn't seem like a very normal thing to say.

"Tinkle?" I said.

"Yeah, you know, go to the restroom?"

"Yeah, I got it," I said, thinking he should have just opened with that.

"I'll be back," he said in a new voice that sounded oddly familiar, then disappeared into the corridor. I looked at Rachel. She just shrugged.

The smell of the food was making me hungry. Rachel sat on one side of the booth, and I sat on the other side. The weird purple vinyl seats oinked as we slid in. A round light fixture hung low above the table, almost too low—like you might bump your head when standing up if you're not careful.

We ate in silence for a few moments.

"So what's your major?" Rachel asked.

I wasn't sure how to answer that. I didn't know how much Ollie had told her about my situation. I hoped not a lot, but she was his girlfriend—he had probably told her at least some things about me. Based on her question, though, it seemed like she didn't know too much.

I squirmed a little in my seat, then quickly blurted out, "I'm undecided," as if I were competing on a game show and had to buzz in my answer before the time limit ran out. I took a bite of my sandwich and then changed the subject. "So when did you learn how to play the piano?"

Rachel wiped her mouth. "Um, I was very young. I was, like, seven when I started playing. My mom was my teacher, and she's a concert pianist, so she started teaching me pretty early on." She started laughing as she continued. "I kind of had to stop having lessons with her, because it's so hard when your parent is your teacher. You kind of just slack off more because you don't have that fear, you know, where you're like, oh my gosh, I haven't practiced! Like, normally, when you don't know someone that well, that's an incentive to practice. So it was hard with my mom, and I think she got fed up with me just, like, messing around."

I laughed, wondering if our own piano lessons are also like that in the future. It was a funny thing to think about. "So when did you, like, start to write your own music?" I asked.

She looked up in thought. "Probably when I was, like, ten or so. At some point, I had kind of discovered that I could make a chord out of three notes, and that's not something my mom really taught me because we were learning classical music. And so I was just, like, kind of fascinated how I could make a tune, and then when I was ten, I think that's when I wrote my first song. I've always loved the way that notes can be combined together in, like, an infinite number of musical possibilities. You know, I kind of look at a piano in, like, the same way a painter probably looks at a blank canvas, or a writer looks at a blank page. Sometimes all those possibilities are overwhelming, but they're really exciting, as well."

There was a sincerity in the way she spoke—a sincerity I wasn't fully reciprocating. But how could I without revealing the truth about me?

"That's awesome," I said. "So, like, what first inspired you to start writing your own stuff?"

"Uh, I don't really know. I was definitely drawn to the piano. I mean, my earliest memory is, like, being in my room and hearing my mom play the piano. Like, I think the sound of the piano is so much a part of me. And I was very drawn to it. But the composing, I don't know. I mean, my dad is an architect, and he's an amazing designer. So maybe the love of creating things came from him."

I wondered how much of this I should have already known. I couldn't shake the feeling that maybe part of the reason I remembered so little about my parents was because, maybe in the future, I don't really care. Maybe I think I already know everything about them. So I don't try to find out more. Maybe I stop being curious at some point. Maybe I'm more concerned about myself than anybody else and care about my issues the most. Maybe that's why I didn't know. The thought haunted me like a sad memory. But that was just it. It wasn't a memory at all that troubled me. Just the opposite. It was the lack of memories. I mean, other than the few vague images of my mom teaching me how to play the piano and my dad teaching me not to be afraid to shoot, I still had no other real knowledge or recollections about my parents.

Ollie returned a moment later from his "wee break" and sat down next to Rachel. They talked about their day, about their classes, about random stuff. I listened and joined in occasionally. They seemed to be genuinely enjoying this. I was enjoying it, too, but then I remembered something:

They're not together in the future.

A pang of sadness stabbed its way through my enjoyment as the realization sunk in. But they seemed...happy? It's not like they were clearly madly in love or anything, but they also didn't look like a couple on the verge of a breakup. If either one of them was unhappy in their relationship, they didn't show it.

After that, every time one of them smiled or laughed at something the other person said, I felt another pang, knowing they wouldn't end up together. I tried to push the thought away. But the more I tried to suppress it, the more I thought about it.

I dropped my spoon into my half-eaten bowl of soup and kept it there, my appetite vanishing like a fleeting dream.

"Hey, you feeling okay, Charlie?" Ollie asked.

"Yeah, I'm fine."

"You gonna eat that?" he asked, pointing to my untouched chocolate chip cookie.

I shook my head. "It's all yours, bro."

"Sweet, thanks, man," he said, grabbing the cookie.

He took a huge bite and started to chew. Then he looked at Rachel and said through a mouthful of food, "Sorry, do you want half?"

"Not anymore," she said with a grin.

I wanted to smile, but something stopped me.

After lunch, we parted ways. Ollie and Rachel both went to their respective classes, and I went...I didn't know. I had to work in the afternoon, but my shift wouldn't start for a few more hours. I thought about going back to Ollie's dorm room, but he had taken his key with him.

So what to do?

My mind was made up for me, as I suddenly realized that I had to—how had Ollie put it? Oh yeah, *tinkle*. I smiled and shook my head at the thought.

I started back down the corridor toward the staircase. When I reached the intersection, I stopped. I didn't remember passing any restrooms on our way to the sandwich shop earlier. I took another look down *that* corridor—the eerie one from before—and sighed. One of those doors had to lead to a restroom, right? I figured what the heck and headed that way.

I heard my footsteps as I moved across the corridor. The chatter at the other end was now a distant murmur. The only other sounds I could hear were water flowing through the white pipes along the ceiling and the buzzing of the dim lights overhead.

I stopped at a door and scanned the corridor. None of the doors seemed to have any signs or markings on them.

Great.

I tried it anyway. Locked. I tried another one. Locked. Then another one.

You guessed it. Locked.

I pushed my shoulder against the door, just in case, but it didn't budge, so I kept moving, running my fingers along the splotchy white wall.

An overhead light flickered. A sudden chill swept through my bones. If I were a ghost, I thought, these walls would be the perfect place to shack up.

So what was I doing here?

Right, I had to pee, or…tinkle.

As I continued down the hallway, I began to feel a bit of déjà vu. Like I had been here before, or, at least, someplace similar to this. But when?

I came across another door. This one was…open? Yes. At least, partially. I pushed the door. It slowly creaked all the way open. I tried to peek in, but it was too dark to tell what was inside.

So I stepped in.

I felt around for a light switch, wishing I had a flashlight on me, and accidentally knocked something over with my hand. It landed with a *thwack*, making me jump. Finally, my hand found a switch. I flicked it on. The space lit up with an eerie yellow glow.

I looked around the dimly lit room. It was a little bigger than I had expected, probably about twice the square footage as Ollie's dorm room. I couldn't tell whether it was an office or some kind of janitorial closet. Maybe both. The place looked like it hadn't been touched in years. Metal shelving units holding brown cardboard boxes lined the cinder-block walls. There was a desk in front of an old-school blackboard. The desk was bare except for a small, long-dead potted plant and an idle fan sitting on top. An orange trash can sat in the middle of the floor, which seemed like an odd spot for a trash can. There were spiderwebs in the corner and a mud stain on the floor—ironically, right next to a mop and yellow bucket. A lone lightbulb hung from the ceiling like a bat. More pipes clung to the ceiling and snaked up and down the walls.

The sight of the room triggered a thought: *I've been here before*.

I was sure of it now. But I didn't know when.

I looked down and saw a broom that I had knocked over at my feet. I picked up the broom and leaned it against the wall. As I did, I noticed something covered in a tarp on my right. I thought it might be another small desk or storage cabinet, but when I pulled the tarp off, I jerked my head back slightly.

Whoa.

It was a piano. No, a keyboard. Like an electronic

keyboard for playing music, not one of those computer keyboards for typing. It was short in length—definitely not a full-size piano with however many keys—but bulky, and old. Or maybe *vintage* would be a better word.

I took a closer look. The keys had yellowed with age, or maybe that was just the lighting. There were lots of knobs and buttons. I didn't know what any of them did. Well, except for one, I guess. I pushed the power button. Then I pressed down on middle C.

Nothing.

I pushed the power button again, in case I had accidentally turned it off the first time, and pressed back down on middle C.

Still nothing.

I figured the keyboard was either broken or not plugged in. I checked for the latter, ducking under the keyboard. Sure enough, I spotted a black power adapter attached to a cable lying on the floor, unplugged. I picked up the adapter and started looking for an outlet in the wall. I found one, right next to the...

Door?

It was small and rusty, almost like an escape hatch. Out of curiosity, I reached for the handle and tried it. Nope. I stepped back. My eyes drifted above the door, to a clock on the wall. I watched as the seconds ticked by.

Tick, tick, tick.

Wait. The clock was ticking...backward?

Tick, tick, tick.

Yep, the hands were moving counterclockwise.

My heart started thumping.

Wait. Could this be…?

I looked back down at the rusty door. Could that door be the portal for time travel? No. That seemed like wishful thinking. I was getting too worked up over a clock that was probably either just malfunctioning or a novelty item. It couldn't be a portal…

Or could it?

I mean, hadn't I already traveled through time? So there had to be a portal or time machine out here somewhere, right? And didn't this room feel familiar? Like I had been here sometime before? Maybe…in the future?

I could feel the hope starting to rise in me now. I had to open that door. But how? I didn't have a clue.

I still had the power adaptor in my hand. I went ahead and plugged it in and returned to the keyboard, standing over the keys since there was no chair. I pushed the power button once again. A red dot lit up on the console.

Bingo.

I tried playing middle C. A soft piano-like sound emitted from the keyboard. I fiddled around with the controls until I found the volume slider. I turned it up, realizing that I probably should have tried adjusting the volume earlier when I was having trouble getting the keyboard to produce any sound.

Then another thought struck me.

What if this keyboard worked like a combination lock? To open a combination lock, you need to turn the dial to the correct sequence of numbers. What if this keyboard worked in the same way? Maybe if I played the correct sequence of notes, the door would unlock. Fat chance, I thought, but it was worth a shot. The question was, what could the sequence be? I searched the room for clues, such as strange symbols on the walls. But I didn't find any. I stopped and tried to think, but nothing came to me.

A faint sound penetrated my thoughts. Music. I listened and could hear the bell tower ringing its now-familiar melody above me. My brain flashed back to when I was watching a rerun of this sitcom called *The King of Queens* with Ollie the other night. In the episode, there was this scene where Doug went to confront the new neighbors about their dog barking and keeping him and his wife, Carrie, up all night. I remembered hearing that same little tune used as…a doorbell.

Wait.

Could it really be that simple?

I rushed back to the keyboard. I couldn't play by ear, so I started pushing random keys, trying to match the notes with the melody ringing throughout the residence hall. I kept striking the keys until I found the right notes. Then I played them all in succession.

G-sharp, E, F-sharp, B…B, F-sharp, G-sharp, E.

I heard a click, and the door creaked open, as though a gust of wind had blown through it.

Whoa.

It had actually worked.

I moved to the door and crouched to see what was beyond it.

Darkness.

Awesome, I thought.

Now I really wished I had a flashlight. I thought for a moment. If that door was the passage that connected the past and the present, the moment I go out this door, would I go back to the year I had come from? Or would I just be thrusted even deeper into the past?

There was only one way to find out.

My heart was pounding like it was about to jump out of my chest. I took a deep breath. Then I slowly ducked under the doorway, disappearing into the dark.

Only I hadn't actually disappeared. I was still in the same place. I kept the door open to let in what little illumination came from the lightbulb on the other side. When my eyes adjusted to the dark, I saw a narrow staircase leading down.

I slowly started down the steps, carefully avoiding the dirt or whatever that was on the grimy steps. The walls were made of concrete and looked just as grungy. My footsteps echoed in the eerily still passageway.

I could actually feel my legs quaking now. I grabbed the wooden handrail on the right in case my legs gave out on me. I took another step and started to feel a funny tingling sensation in my fingertips. Buzzy. Was there some kind of electrical current flowing through the railing? Can currents even travel through wood?

Either way, I jerked my hand away from the railing as though I had just touched a hot stove. But it didn't really help. I went down another step, extending my hands to the side, and pressed hard against the wall on both sides as if the passageway was closing in on me. Really, I was just trying not to fall on my face in the darkness.

Both my arms were tingling now. I could feel the sensation starting to move across my body. It was such a strange feeling.

My heart kicked into an even higher gear. I took another step forward. The tingling sensation was sweeping up and down me now, like a wave. My body was almost vibrating.

What the heck was happening to me?

I went down with my right foot. Went down with my left foot, and all at once a bucket of memories from my life in the future poured over me, like cold water.

I fell back and used my hands to brace myself as my butt landed on a step behind me. It was hardly a fall. But I felt as though I had just plummeted from fifty feet into a spike trap as a horrible realization from the future hit me:

Ollie dies in an accident while he and my mom are still dating.

CHAPTER 12

I turned around and raced back up the steps, as though I had just seen a monster at the bottom of the staircase. In a way, I sort of did.

The Monster of Death.

Only the monster wasn't coming for me. It was coming for my friend.

But what exactly happens to Ollie anyway? What kind of accident is it? And when does it happen?

The tingling sensation quickly faded as I went back into the room and slammed the door shut behind me. I couldn't go back to the future. Not yet.

My memory was still hazy. I still didn't remember a lot of details about my life, or especially the accident. I didn't even know how I knew about it in the first place. My memories were all scrambled.

But I knew.

Same way I knew Rachel was my mom. Same way I knew Robbie was my dad.

Mom must have been so heartbroken. The thought felt like another gut punch, breaking me into pieces.

And then another dark thought invaded my mind:

If Mom and Dad don't end up together, I won't...be born.

Say I find a way to prevent the accident from happening...then what? Do I try to break him and Rachel apart? Make up a lie or pit them against each other in an attempt to drive a wedge between them? Maybe I should just go back and let things play out as they are meant to. Maybe I shouldn't try to change things.

Stop it, I scolded myself.

I couldn't waste this opportunity. I needed to find out when Ollie got into the accident and prevent it from happening, no matter the cost. I'll change his future. That's the reason I traveled to the year 2008.

I looked around me. The room looked exactly the same as before. *Good*, I thought. I hadn't gone back yet.

Or had I?

That tingly feeling was replaced with fear taking over my body. I bolted out of the room. When I reached the intersection, I turned right, darted across the hallway, and sprinted up the spiral staircase, passing a few confused— and probably annoyed—students along the way.

As I headed into the main entryway, I heard a voice say, "Yo, Charlie!"

I stopped and spun around. The voice belonged to

Ronnie, who was sitting at the front desk. He looked the same as when I had first met him the other day. I relaxed a little, relieved that I hadn't jumped to the future or slipped further into the past.

"Hey," I said. I walked over to him and now saw that he was eating a donut.

"You good?" he asked before taking another bite.

"Yeah," I said, rubbing the back of my head for some reason. "I just...have to go to the restroom."

"There's one past the lounge over there," he said, pointing to my left.

I looked that way and said, "Thanks."

"No problem. You going to Ollie's play tomorrow?"

"Yeah. You?"

He nodded. "Yeah."

"I'll see you there," I said, starting to walk away.

"Talk to you later, bro."

I went to the restroom, then headed back up to the top floor and sat on the sofa in the common area, waiting for Ollie to come back. Suehan—the Korean computer science major—and two other guys I didn't know the names of were chatting about their favorite professional soccer players. I didn't know anything about soccer, but I tried to join in on their conversation to distract myself. I kept glancing down the hallway every time I heard footsteps, hoping to see Ollie marching down the hallway with his signature power walk, but he never showed.

A few hours later, I headed over to DiVincenzo's for my shift at work. I got there several minutes early. As I made my way to the kitchen, I stopped walking, dead in my tracks. There, emerging from the kitchen doors right in front of me, was Ollie.

He smiled when he saw me. "Hey, what's up, man?"

Without thinking, I ran up to him and hugged him hard.

He grunted in surprise, like I had just knocked the wind out of him. "Whoa. Unexpected PDA there, bro." He slid his arm around and patted me on the back. "But, uh…hey, love you, too, man."

After pulling out of the hug, I looked at him. He was wearing a black vest over a white dress shirt, and a bow tie. He was also carrying his puffer jacket.

"What are you doing here?" I asked.

"I work here, remember? I started my shift after my last class."

"Right."

He studied me for a moment. "You got a weird look in your eyes, man. Are you all right?"

"I need to talk to you."

"Well, I'd love to stay and chat, but I have to get going," he said, slipping on his jacket.

"Wait. Where are you going?"

He zipped up his jacket. "Rehearsal. I got off early so I could make it in time."

I wanted to go with him, but I was just about to start my own shift. I couldn't just let him leave though without saying anything.

"Ollie, listen to me." I put my hands on his shoulders and turned him to face me. "You need to be careful from now on. Don't stay out late or do anything stupid. I'll stay by your side as much as possible, but I need you to be safe."

"Huh? Where's all this coming from?"

"Please, just be safe."

"I'll be so safe," he said in a jokey voice.

"No, I'm serious, man!" I snapped, my patience wearing thin. "I'm not messing around." I needed to express the gravity of the situation to him, so I got a little more direct and said, "Something bad is gonna happen to you if you're not careful."

"What are you talking about?"

Man, how do I explain this?

I know your future, I wanted to say, *and I'm trying to change your fate. You will get into an accident. Because of that, you will die, and I must prevent it from happening, no matter what.*

Instead, I went with, "I know it's hard to believe, and I can't really explain it…So could you just have faith in me and listen to me?"

Ollie pulled away. "I gotta get going, man. I don't wanna be late. We'll talk later."

I wanted to stop him, but I couldn't. I knew how important this play was to him, and the truth was, I had no idea when or where the accident would happen. It could be any second. And that's what scared me.

I watched until he vanished out the door.

I worried about Ollie all evening. As soon as my shift ended, I went straight back to the dorm. To my surprise, Ollie was already in bed, the lights turned out. Relieved, I took a shower, then climbed straight into my bunk.

As I was lying there in the darkness, I could hear a group of guys chatting and laughing outside Ollie's door. Same thing every night. Kind of wished Ollie's dorm room wasn't right by the common area. But whatever. It's not like I was about to fall asleep anyway with everything that was on my mind.

The heat kicked on, the vent blowing warm air into the room.

"Hey, Ollie, you up?" I said quietly, but not too quietly so he could hear me.

"Yeah," he said, which surprised me. "What's up?"

I wanted to warn him again, make sure I got through to him, but I knew that he had a lot on his mind already with opening night of his play happening tomorrow. So I decided to stay away from it.

"So, you nervous for the big show tomorrow?" I asked instead, rolling onto my side.

"I am now," he joked.

I laughed. "You want me to help you practice your lines or something?"

"Oh, no. I am maxed out. Gotta save myself for the big show. You know?"

"Yeah, I feel you." I paused. "So, why'd you get into acting anyway? Was it to get rich and famous?"

He puffed out a snort of laughter. "Nah, man. If I did it for the money, I would've quit years ago. I mean, the second I started acting, I knew that I loved it. But I don't think I ever thought I would do it professionally because it's just such a hard job. Even at eight years old, I knew how unrealistic it was to become an actor and how cutthroat the industry could be. I'm not naive, and I know that there are kids all over the world doing exactly what I'm doing, loving it just as much. But it's my dream. It's what I want to do. Gotta at least try. You know?"

"For sure. So, like, what are your plans after you graduate?"

"I'm still figuring it out. But all signs point me to New York."

"You'd really move out to New York?"

"Yeah, I love New York so much. I just went there last summer, and I met so many like-minded artists there. I feel like everybody is going there to seriously pursue their art. Life happens so randomly in New York. You have to plan so heavily in most places. In New York, you can just walk outside and for ten hours, your day is made, and you're having fun. So just…New York's happening. I love it there. I also just love theater, and there's theater galore there."

I propped myself up on an elbow. "So what do you like about theater so much?"

Even though I couldn't see him, I could feel his enthusiastic smile. "Ah, man, theater is so beautiful. I just love the energy of theater. I love the fact that we go from beginning to end consecutively. You know, you never redo it. I love the beauty of how the show must go on, and I love being in front of an audience, and they laugh or cry with you. And you feel that energy in real time, and it feeds you. And then seeing your friends afterward. And also just the feeling of being backstage, I love so much. While the show is going on, running into the darkness, knowing that you're there for your cast members, and they're there for you. Theater is just so amazing."

He paused, then added, "But I also want to get into working on movies and shows. LA is better for that sort of thing, but New York also has a lot of great opportunities for film and TV, even though theater is what most actors are there for. But yeah, I'm looking forward to trying new things."

"That's awesome, man," I said, trying to hide the anguish in my voice. Hearing him talk with so much excitement about the future hurt in the worst way, knowing he'd never get the opportunity to pursue those things unless I found a way to change his fate.

I heard Ollie shift in his bed. "What about you, man? What's your wild dream?"

"Me?"

"Yeah."

I considered the question. I thought about the way I'd felt playing the piano after watching Mom play the other day, the way I'd felt with the basketball in my hands when rebounding for Dad. Were those just my parents' dreams? Or were they mine, too?

I shook my head, even though he couldn't see me. "I don't know, man."

"Well, you're still alive, right? You must have something to live for, too."

"Yeah, I guess you're right."

The room fell quiet. I rolled onto my back, put my hands behind my head, and stared up at the ceiling in the dark. "You know, you never answered my question the other day," I said.

"What question?"

"Why did you help me? I mean, weren't you a little worried I was gonna, like, rob you or something when you let me crash with you?"

"Rob me?"

"Yeah, you know, like, steal your movie collection, or your shoe collection or something."

"Huh."

"What?"

"Nothing. It's just…you make a good point. I honestly didn't even think about that. Maybe I shouldn't have helped you," he joked.

I laughed. "So why did you?"

Ollie was quiet for a few moments. Long enough that I started to wonder if he had fallen asleep. But then he spoke. "Because you were in trouble, I guess. I don't know. I wanted to help. You know, it just seemed like you needed help, so I helped. It really wasn't that deep. It just felt like the right thing to do." He paused. "And as the great Albus Dumbledore once said"—he started speaking in a deep and somewhat gravelly voice—"'We must all face the choice between what is right and what is easy.'"

I smiled. Neither of us said anything again for a while. I was thinking about what that quote meant when I started hearing a siren wailing in the distance. A minute or so passed before it faded away.

"Ollie?"

"Yeah?"

"I'm really glad I got to meet you."

It felt kind of weird saying it out loud randomly like that, but I guess it's easier saying things in the dark where it's like only your words exist. And I've said this before, but without him, where would I be?

"Thanks, Charlie," he said. "That means a lot. And I'm really glad I met you, too."

Everything felt okay for a moment, even though it wasn't.

I wanted to keep talking, keep pushing back the dark, but I could feel my eyelids drooping. So I let them. I closed my eyes for a moment. I thought back to what Ollie had said about helping me, and then I thought about his own fate yet again and what was at stake. I could feel the weight of responsibility bearing down on my shoulders. It was an obligation. Not choice—responsibility. I couldn't turn away, even if I wanted to.

I had a mission. And I had to succeed, even if I risked my life.

CHAPTER 13

When I entered the theater the next evening, the place was packed.

You ask me, a big reason for that was my boy, Ollie Jones. Or, Oliver Jones, as he was listed in the program. It seemed like half the top floor of Reinhart had shown up to support Ollie. I didn't know whether Ollie had scored them all tickets or they had gotten them on their own. Either way, I spotted a lot of familiar faces.

It was only a few minutes to showtime. I sat next to Ronnie toward the end of the row and looked around at the nearly full auditorium. The theater was located on the edge of campus, next to another large venue and not far from DiVincenzo's. I had actually walked by it before without realizing it. I had made sure to request not to work this evening so I could go see the play.

The lights faded out.

Showtime.

The stage was dark. There was a moment of silence.

Then light came up revealing a young man with long greased hair sitting in a living area, wearing blue jeans and a T-shirt. And the show began.

A few minutes into the play, Ollie's character—I knew his name was Dallas Winston from the program and what Ollie had told me—made his first appearance, rushing onstage after the main character, Ponyboy—I still thought that was a funny name—got jumped by a bunch of dudes in some gang and had a knife pulled on him.

Ollie's character, Dallas, was sporting unruly hair, dark blue jeans, and a leather bomber jacket, as well as a necklace. He was also smoking a fake cigarette and spoke in that same New York accent I'd heard in the car ride the other day when he was pretending to drive me to the hospital.

It was kind of weird hearing him talk like that and seeing him act all tough and angry. Apparently, in the play, Dallas had just gotten out of jail, and he was acting kind of like a jerk in some of the early scenes, which was totally different from the Ollie I knew. Despite that, he played the part naturally and with nuance. I *believed* him. I mean, in the moment, I didn't feel like I was watching him act. It felt like he *was* that character. I guess that meant he was a good actor. It was like he had turned into a whole new person.

Partway through the play, the lights came up for intermission. Phones came out, and chatter filled the air. All

around the auditorium, people rose, stretched, and headed for the restrooms or concession stand.

"I'm gonna get something to eat," Ronnie said to me
as he slid out of the row. "You want anything?"

"Nah, I'm good," I said. "But thanks."

After Ronnie left, I shifted in my seat. Stretched my
legs a bit. I felt kind of awkward just sitting there with
everyone around me leaving, so even though I didn't
have a reason to, I got up and wandered into the lobby
area. A bunch of framed photos and posters of past
performances adorned the green walls. I studied some of
them for a few moments, then turned around and
stopped when I saw someone I recognized.

It was Mom, aka Rachel, aka—my personal favorite—
Hemorrhoid.

She wore a floral dress and brown ankle boots and was
talking to a group of people. I waited for their conversation to end, then approached her.

She smiled when she saw me and gave a little wave.
"Hey, Charlie! Good to see you."

"Hey, Mom—I mean, hey, Rachel."

I wanted to smack myself on the side of the head, or
maybe ram my head into the wall. I couldn't believe I had
slipped and actually called her Mom. I mean, she *was* my
mom. So it wasn't *that* weird. But can you imagine what
it would be like if you accidentally called one of your
friends Mom? Or Dad?

Yeah. Awkward.

Luckily, the chatter was loud enough that I don't think she'd really heard me.

"Thanks for coming!" she said. "Ollie was really glad you could make it."

"Yeah, no problem. It's cool seeing Ollie do his thing. I didn't know how good of an actor he was. I mean, I've seen him do impressions before. But seeing him on stage is crazy."

She nodded and brushed a strand of hair out of her eyes. "Yeah, he's definitely in his element."

"For sure."

A man and a woman came up next to Rachel. She glanced at them, then back to me.

"Oh, right. Charlie, this is my mom and dad. Mom and Dad, this is Charlie. He's Ollie's new roommate."

I looked at them, and it took a moment or two for it to click.

Grandpa and Grandma.

Mr. Murphy—Grandpa—had graying hair and a goatee. He wore a dress shirt, khakis, and glasses. Mrs. Murphy—Grandma—had brown hair that flowed down to about her shoulders. She also wore glasses, along with earrings and a black dress.

They both smiled at me and shook my hand. I wanted to hug them—I mean, they were my grandparents after all—but I couldn't. They didn't know me yet. I tried to remember them, and when I couldn't, I morbidly wondered whether they are still alive in the future. The thought made me want to hug them even more.

After shaking hands, I looked at them both and said, "Your daughter's, like, insanely talented at the keys, by the way. I mean, I heard her play the piano the other day and was super impressed."

They both smiled proudly.

"We're very proud of her," Mr. Murphy said.

"Do you play any instruments?" Mrs. Murphy asked me.

I stuffed both hands into my pockets. "Uh, yeah, I play the piano a little bit. I'm not nearly as good as Rachel"—I cast a quick glance at her—"but I have a good teacher, so hopefully, I'll keep getting better."

"Who's your teacher?" Mrs. Murphy asked.

Boy, I had really backed myself into a corner, huh?

I fidgeted nervously and started to panic, but then I realized that I could still tell the truth and not give away anything revealing about my relation to them. "Uh, it's my mom."

She smiled. "Oh, that's wonderful. I also taught Rachel growing up. We still have a lesson every now and then, but to be honest, I think she's outgrown me." She started laughing. "She should be giving *me* lessons now."

I laughed and wanted to keep talking to them, but the lights overhead started flashing to let the audience know to head back in, so I returned to my seat for the second act.

I mentioned before that the character Ollie was portraying—Dallas Winston—seemed tough and mean. And he was. But as the play went on, he started showing a softer side, and I started to warm up to him a bit. Toward the end of the first act, he had helped Ponyboy and Johnny find a safe hiding place in an abandoned church when they were in trouble and gave them money and dry clothes. In the second act, he continued to look out for them, and he even recklessly put his life on the line and rescued his friends from the collapse of a burning building in this scene where the church was on fire.

I remembered Ollie saying something to me the other day about how his goal when playing any character is to find all the ways in which they're similar. I think that, generally, he was very different from the character Dallas. But Dallas risking his life to protect his friends and keep them out of trouble showed his loyalty and compassion, which were traits I could see in Ollie, one hundred percent.

I started thinking about Ollie's accident in the future. I wondered if maybe that's how he dies—protecting someone else. I wondered whether or not I would be willing to do the same thing, even for a stranger.

Turned out, Ollie had been right. The play was definitely a tear-jerker. Not that I started crying or anything.

Okay, I might have gotten a little misty-eyed at one point, but no tears were shed. In my defense, the ending of the play was, like, the saddest thing in the world.

The lights dimmed out, and the audience started clapping. After a few moments, the lights came up again, and the cast members trotted out to the front of the stage in pairs and groups to acknowledge the applause and took bows.

There was a chain-link fence on stage used as a prop during the show. The other cast members simply walked in front of the fence when they came out. Ollie, however, stayed in character and hopped the fence on his way to the front of the stage and received roaring applause as he took a bow and waved to the audience in appreciation.

I felt like a proud parent as I stood and cheered with the other spectators while watching Ollie soak up all the love from the audience. I wanted to shout, *That's my roommate!* or something like that but way less corny to let the people know. But there was a feeling in the pit of my stomach I couldn't shake.

I went backstage after the show to meet up with Ollie. The air smelled like dust, paint, and wood. The place looked kind of like a workshop, with tall wooden structures, as well as a flimsy staircase. Ladders leaned against the wall. There were racks of costumes and various props and artifacts lying around on the floor.

As I waited, I helped myself to some of the free refreshments sitting on a table and talked with Rachel and a few of the guys from Reinhart who had stuck around. Unfortunately, Rachel's parents had to leave, so I didn't get to visit with them more like I was hoping to.

Eventually, Ollie emerged from one of the rooms and made his way over, a huge smile on his face. Pure joy and elation. Hugs all around. I could see how much he was enjoying this. I was enjoying it, too. But that feeling in the pit of my stomach never left.

The room slowly started to fizzle out as people left. Rachel was the last one in Ollie's posse to leave, other than me. I was planning to walk back to the dorm with Ollie, so I stayed the entire time. Ollie and Rachel hugged goodbye one last time and went their separate ways.

I followed after Ollie. "That was sick, man," I said for probably the third or fourth time. "You were amazing."

He smiled, and I wondered if his cheeks were starting to hurt from all the smiling. "Thanks, man." He put his arm around me. "Means a lot."

We stepped outside. A rush of cold air stung my face. My breath puffed out in front of me. Felt like winter was on the horizon. I regretted not bringing a jacket or coat, but then I realized I didn't even have either of those. I dug my hands into my pockets and looked up at the sky. Clouds blotted out the moon and the stars.

It was pretty late, but people were still out and about. A group of sorority girls laughed at something funny one of them said. A little boy trotted with a red balloon in front of a woman who I assumed was his mom. An old man sat on a bench, either waiting for a ride or lost.

We stopped at a crosswalk. I stood at the front of a group of people, with Ollie on my right, and stared impatiently at the light, trying to will it to change so I could get out of the cold pronto. Cars drove by, a blend of engine sounds, tire noise, and the thumping of bass filling the night air. A gust of wind hit our backs.

And that was when the balloon slipped out of the little boy's fingers, and he suddenly ran out into the street as another car approached.

"Zachary, no!" a woman shouted behind me.

And then it hit me.

This was it.

This was the moment everything would change.

In less than a flash, Ollie would jump onto the street and try to save that little boy's life.

But end up losing his own, sacrificing himself.

That's the kind of person he was—the kind who would run into a burning building to save his friends—or even a total stranger in this case. Ollie knew that car was going to hit the little boy, killing him. He had to do something.

As a result, one of the happiest nights of Ollie's life…would end up being the last night of his life.

I had to change that.

I had to find a way to change history and protect them both, even if it meant...

What was that Dumbledore quote again?

"We must all face the choice between what is right and what is easy."

Ollie had already started to make his move. It was now or never. I jerked to the right, knocking Ollie off balance. He went down on the sidewalk. I jumped onto the street—no hesitation—and dove for the little boy, shoving him out of the way. I fell hard to the ground, slamming my chest and chin on the pavement. Adrenaline kept the pain at bay, but the air got knocked out of me. I couldn't breathe. Like I had plunged into a murky lake and couldn't find the surface.

I tried to roll away, but when I looked up, I was staring into two starbursts of headlights.

And that's the last thing I remember.

23 YEARS LATER

CHAPTER 14

There are moments in life that can alter—no, shatter—your perception of reality.

It's like one moment, you're looking in the same mirror you've walked in front of every day of your life. Then the next moment, with your eyes still locked on your reflection—*BAM!*—someone fires a bullet. Not at you, but at the mirror. And the glass breaks into a million little pieces.

Or maybe it's actually the opposite. Like all this time, you've been looking at your reflection in a cracked mirror, seeing a fragmented version of yourself. And now the broken pieces have finally slid into place, just like a puzzle, and you're looking at yourself in a new and unsettling way.

I was sitting there on the floor, trying to figure out what was happening, when I started to realize something.

Have you ever had a vivid dream growing up that stuck with you? Say you had a dream that took place in a big white building with huge windows all around. Then one day, you happen to drive by a building that looks just like the one in your dream, even though you've never been there or seen it before. At this point, you might be thinking, well, there are a lot of big white buildings with huge windows in the world. Maybe it just reminds you of the building in your dream. And, yeah, that might very well be the case. But the architecture of this building is exactly the same as you remember from your dream. Even the smallest details, like a staircase wrapping around the building or a large flag hanging in the entryway, match your dream perfectly.

That was what this was like.

In my dream, I had gone back in time and met my parents when they were in college and befriended Ollie Jones.

If that name doesn't ring any bells, you might be living under a rock. He's a big-time actor who's best known for his starring role in a fantasy series about—get this—a time-traveling wizard. He graduated from Barkley University, so he's pretty much royalty in this town. Rumor had it that he might be back in town this week.

Like a lot of dreams, I woke up right before I was about to...

I shuddered at the thought, breathing in short, sharp bursts. In my head, it had always been just that—a dream. But now, as I sat on the floor and looked up at the old keyboard again in the room that served as either an office or janitorial closet—or maybe something far more mysterious—I started thinking maybe it wasn't a dream.

Maybe…it was real.

My head spun. *What's going on? Whose memories are these? Am I hallucinating? Or having a fever dream? I feel so…*

I put a hand to my forehead, as if that would somehow stop my head from spinning like an out-of-control carousel. My mind was caught in a web of memories that were so vivid and yet felt like another lifetime. I tried to ground myself in what I knew for certain. Okay, my name is Charlie Benson. I'm the son of Robbie and Rachel Benson. I'm a freshman at Barkley University, where I play basketball and am coached by my dad.

I took a deep breath, tried to let it out real slow, and looked around me. The old room felt frozen in time, looking exactly as it did more than twenty years ago.

To think, just a few minutes ago, I was simply looking for a restroom. And now, I was questioning everything…

And still looking for a restroom.

My phone buzzed, interrupting my thoughts. It was a text from my mom, telling me that she was parked outside my dorm with my new piano keyboard that had finally been delivered.

My mom is a piano composer and taught me how to play. I love music. Creating, performing, producing, mixing and mastering—the whole process. I think that came from her. I've been producing and writing music in my bedroom for almost five years now and would love to make a career out of it. I know that's probably not really realistic and the odds aren't rooting for me, but like a good friend of mine once said…gotta try, right?

I got up and went out the door, leaving the arcane room behind.

When I first moved into Reinhart Hall at the start of the fall semester, I had a strange feeling that I had been here before. Like one of those dreams I described before. Now, I realized that I had been right all along. I *had* been here before. But the inside was completely renovated, making it hard to recognize. The dining hall from back then didn't even exist anymore and had been replaced by a bigger one across the street.

I joined the small crowd of students flowing in and out of the building and stepped outside. The crisp fall air felt nice. Like opening a fridge door on a hot summer day.

My mom was waiting by the car in one of the metered slots out front, the trunk popped open. The wind blew her hair across her face. "Hi, Charlie," she said, moving the hair out of her eyes.

"Hey, Mom." I looked inside the trunk at a long cardboard box wrapped in an old blanket. "Thanks for bringing this over."

"Of course."

I knew she was happy to do it. In fact, I didn't even have to ask her. She always loved the idea of me playing the piano. It was something we both enjoyed.

I started to lift the box out of the trunk. My mom helped.

"Do you want me to help you carry it inside?" she asked after we set it down on the ground.

"No, I got it," I quickly said, not wanting the embarrassment of having my mommy help me carry something that wasn't even that heavy back to my dorm room.

"You sure?"

"Yeah, I'm fine. Thanks."

She didn't seem totally satisfied with my answer, but she moved on. "Okay. Bye, Charlie. Love you," she said, wrapping me in a hug.

I resisted at first—I mean, there were other students around, and it was a little embarrassing. But then I flashed back to how I'd felt all those years ago when I wanted to hug my mom after recognizing her but couldn't because she didn't know who I was at the time. And so I hugged her back and let her hold me a little longer than usual.

"Love you, too."

She wished me luck on my basketball game that night, and then she drove off.

I lifted the box, which suddenly felt a lot heavier than before, and started back toward the old dorm building. I didn't know which was crazier to believe—that I had traveled through time, or that this building was somehow still standing. I looked at the four white pillars and the large unlit lantern hanging above the door.

Trashy, but classy, I thought.

I think I finally got what Ollie had meant by that.

My arms were starting to get tired when I heard a male voice behind me say, "Hey, excuse me, sir?"

I turned around and saw a middle-aged dude wearing sunglasses and a Barkley baseball cap. He had a short dark brown beard and was with a teenage girl who I assumed was his daughter.

"Sorry to bother you," the man went on, "but I haven't been to campus in a while, and it's changed a lot since I was last here. Do you know where the admissions office is?"

I dropped the box and pointed to my left. "Turn right at the stop sign over there, and it's the first building past the plaza."

He didn't say anything. Just gave me a weird look, like he was studying me. He took off his sunglasses and started making his way toward me, still staring a hole in me. The girl—looking confused—followed.

"Sorry," he finally said, "I don't mean to stare. I just...You look a lot like somebody I used to know, and...what's your name?"

"I'm Charlie," I said, holding out my hand.

His eyes widened, and he took a half step back. "What…did you say your name was?"

"Uh, Charlie," I said again, confused.

"Charlie…Benson?"

"Yeah," I said, surprised. Did I know this guy?

Wait. That face…

He shook his head. "No, this has gotta be a prank or something, or maybe I'm hallucinating." He turned toward the girl. "Are you seeing this?"

She nodded. "Uh-huh."

He turned his gaze back on me. "Whoa, this is like some *Pirates of the Caribbean* action."

I think it was in that moment I knew.

He looked me up and down. "Are you a ghost? Or…a zombie?"

"No," I said flatly. "I'm actually an alien." I pointed to a random car parked in the street. "My spaceship's parked right over there."

He gasped, seeing it now. "Oh my gosh, it *is* you…"

I looked at him. "Ollie…?"

He nodded slowly. Then he threw his arms around me and gave me the meanest bear hug of my life, nearly tackling me.

I grunted in surprise. "Whoa. Unexpected PDA there, bro," I said, using his own line from all those years ago on him.

He laughed through tears. "I watched you die, man."

I could feel tears forming in my eyes now, too. "I know," I said solemnly. "I'm sorry."

We finally pulled apart.

Ollie wiped away his tears and studied my face. "You haven't aged a day, man."

"What about you? You don't look a day over sixty," I joked.

He laughed. Then he stared at me again. "But...how?"

"I have a lot to tell you, man."

Ollie turned toward the girl next to him. "Oh, sorry, where are my manners?" He put his arm around her. "This is my daughter. Charlie, meet...Charlie."

We shook hands.

"Cool name," I said, smiling.

"Thanks," she said, returning my smile. "I've heard a lot about you."

Ollie wiped his eyes again. "We named her after the guy who saved a little boy's life—not to mention the kid who ran into the street."

We all laughed for a few moments, and then Ollie checked the time on his watch. "Oh, shoot, we have to get going." His eyes shifted to the other Charlie. "This one has her first official college visit. Don't want to be late for the tour."

I also had class coming up, so we exchanged numbers and agreed to meet up for coffee later.

* * *

A few hours later, Ollie was ordering a medium latte at New Horizon, a trendy coffee shop downtown. I ordered a small coffee. Charlie—his daughter—was meeting with a friend who lived in the area, according to Ollie.

Word must have spread that Ollie Jones was on campus. There was a small crowd of people—mostly students—wanting to get a photo taken with him. Ollie agreed to all of them and even signed a few autographs.

After getting our drinks, we sat at a small high-top table by the window. The chairs had spindly little legs that screeched when I awkwardly tried to scoot forward in mine. I would have rather sat in a booth tucked away, but I have to admit, the high-top table felt more regal. Or maybe that's just because I was sitting with a celebrity.

I took a sip of the coffee. It was bitter, but that's how I like it. Way I see it, the less you need, the better off you are. "So what's it like to be famous?" I asked.

Ollie stirred a packet of sugar into his latte. "It's all right."

"But...?" I said, because I could sense he was holding back.

He thought for a moment, like he was searching for the right words. "It's weird."

"What do you mean?"

He fiddled with his cup a little, then looked at me again. "I mean, one day you're not famous, and then suddenly, you are. And the weird thing is that, like, in your head, you know that nothing has really changed. I mean, I'm still the same person that I was before. All the things that mattered to me before still matter to me now. But everyone looks at you differently."

I glanced around at the people staring at our table. "Yeah, I guess that makes sense."

"So," Ollie said after taking a sip, "you want to tell me how the heck you came back from the dead?"

I didn't even know where to start. Finally, I said, "So...you remember Rachel Murphy?"

He nodded as he took another sip. "Yeah."

"Well...she's my mom," I said, dropping bomb number one on him.

He froze as he was about to set his cup down, and I could see the shock in his eyes. His face twisted in confusion as he tried to sort through it. "Hold up...What?"

"You remember when we first met, like, twenty-some years ago?"

He nodded. "Yeah."

"I had come from the future," I said, dropping bomb number two.

He cocked an eyebrow. "Are you messing with me, Charlie?"

"No."

"'Cause I feel like you're messing with me."

"I'm dead serious, man. I swear." I told him about the office/janitorial closet in the basement of Reinhart, the old keyboard, the clock that ticked backward, and the small door. Then I told him how I knew something bad would happen to him and I had to find a way to prevent it from happening.

At first, I thought he still wouldn't believe me. But the thing was, like he said, he'd watched me die. And yet I was sitting right in front of him now. There really was no logical explanation that would have made any more sense than the truth.

When I finished, he lifted his cap and ran a hand through his hair. "You know, in a weird way, that actually kind of makes sense. I mean, after you…the police went through your belongings, and they found your IDs from the future."

"So what happened?"

"It was actually a pretty big story. Most people thought it was fake or Photoshopped."

"What about you?"

"Honestly, I was ninety-nine percent sure the story was a hoax. Probably just a typo or fake ID or someone trolling. But there was still that one-percent chance it could be true. And now…" His voice trailed off.

We fell into silence for a moment or two. Then I said, "Hey, can I ask you something personal?"

"Sure."

I hesitated before saying, "What happened with you and Mom—I mean, you and Rachel?"

"That's a fair question," he said with a nod. "Nothing bad happened. I feel like that's often an assumption that people make when two people break up. She's a great woman, but we just weren't working at the time. Our lives were just going in two different directions, and it wasn't really anything we could help. It's just how the cookie crumbled, as the saying goes."

"So…are you married?"

He nodded. "Yeah. I met my wife while doing theater in New York, and we've been married for almost twenty years. She's back home in New York with our other daughter."

"That's awesome, man."

I checked the time on my phone. I wanted to keep talking for hours, but it was time for me to go to Hayward Fieldhouse for a pregame team meeting and shoot-around.

"Sorry, man, I have to get going," I said, standing up. "I have a basketball game tonight."

"You're on Barkley's basketball team?" he said, his voice laced with surprise.

"Yeah, dude. I actually tried to get you last-minute tickets in case you wanted to go, but they're all sold out."

He smiled and slipped out two tickets. "Way ahead of you, buddy." He paused. "To be honest, I've been so busy, I haven't really been following Barkley basketball lately. But Charlie really likes basketball, and so I thought it would be a good father-daughter bonding opportunity, you know?"

"Yeah, for sure." I grabbed my empty cup. "Cool. I'll see you there, man."

"Good luck, Charlie."

"Thanks, man."

We hugged goodbye and went our separate ways.

Music blasted from the speakers in the gym. It was almost game time.

After doing a weave layup drill, my dad—Barkley's head coach—emerged from the tunnel, with the same short, curly black hair from before, only maybe a little less now, and a few strands of gray.

"Hey, Coach!" I called out to him.

He came over and hugged me. "Good to see you, Son. You be aggressive tonight. Play hard, all right?"

"I will."

Pretty soon, our team headed to our bench. As I made my way over, I glanced cross-court at Ollie standing courtside with Charlie.

He smiled when he saw me and made a pretend hoop with his arms, like we were back in the hallway on the top floor of Reinhart.

I pretended to dribble an invisible basketball, crossed up an imaginary defender, and then put up the J.

Ollie looked up and swung his arms to his right, as if

he had to move the hoop for the shot to drop, and then flashed another wide smile and gave me two big thumbs up.

Bang, I thought, imagining the ball sailing through the hoop. *And the crowd goes wild.*

It might not have been real, but the feeling still was.

CHAPTER 15

A few days later, I found myself hiking a trail with Ollie at one of the nearby state parks under a cold November sky. Ollie wouldn't tell me where we were going, but I followed him anyway.

Wind rustled through the branches of the trees, their remaining leaves glistening with droplets of water that shimmered in the fading sunlight. Some of the fallen leaves crunched under our feet, while others had already been smashed and were embedded in the soil.

The trail winded through an endless canopy of trees. It was pretty beautiful, I have to admit. But I still had no idea what we were doing out here.

"Are you sure you know where we're going?" I asked Ollie.

He looked back at me and motioned for me to follow him. "Yes. Come on. This way."

Most hikes I'd previously been on—which, granted, weren't very many—were a nice balance of uphills and downhills. But this one seemed to perpetually climb upward. We'd only been hiking a few minutes, and my lungs and legs were already starting to burn. I thought I was in pretty good shape. But I guess hiking shape must be different from basketball shape.

Ollie seemed to have no problems with the hills, though, even with his joints being twenty-some years older than mine. He deftly hopped from rock to rock and zigzagged across the uneven terrain.

"You're not taking me to the hospital, are you?" I joked. Well, mostly joked.

Ollie shook his head. "Man, after all these years, you still don't want to go to the hospital." He slipped behind a tree.

I followed. "Are you taking me somewhere to kill me, then?"

He hesitated. "No, but…"

I stopped. "But what?"

"You'll see. Come on. We're almost there."

My curiosity piqued, I walked ahead of Ollie and channeled my inner Bear Grylls as I strode through the trees. As we walked by a grassy open area on the left, I felt a tap on my arm. I turned around. "Now what?"

Ollie was gazing at the small clearing in front of us. But then I saw several wooden crosses and headstones scattered across the glade and realized that it wasn't actually an empty field.

It was a cemetery.

I looked in front of me and felt my blood go cold when I saw it.

What the...?

There, in the middle of the old cemetery, was a small headstone with the following epitaph: IN MEMORY OF CHARLIE BENSON.

I read it once, then again, still struggling to wrap my head around it.

The headstone was gray and starting to look old and worn. A pile of brown leaves rested at the base. There were no drawings or decorations on the headstone. Just those five little words that shook me to my core. I felt my entire body shudder when I thought about my own lifeless body being buried six feet underground.

Talk about unnerving.

For a long time, neither of us said anything. We just stood there in thoughtful silence.

The leaves rustled on the ground and then scattered as a gentle breeze blew past.

Finally, I broke the silence. "Is that...?"

Ollie nodded. "Yeah." He looked at me. "Pretty wild, huh?"

"No kidding."

Another beat of silence, then: "I'm glad you're alive, Charlie."

I looked at him. "I'm glad you're alive, too, Ollie."

It was a strange thing to say to someone. Basically, *Hey, glad you're not dead.* The kind of thing that normally goes without saying. But maybe it's okay to say those things sometimes. It never hurts to be reminded that we matter to someone. Plus, in a way, we both should have been dead, so maybe it wasn't that weird.

My eyes drifted to the other headstones and grave markings in the area, and it got me thinking about life and death.

The truth is, no one knows how much time they will have on this earth. All we can do is make the most of the time we're given.

After a while, Ollie turned to me. "Come on, there's something else I want to show you."

I shook my head. "I think I've had enough surprises for one day."

He grinned. "No, trust me, you're gonna want to see this." He headed back up the trail, and I followed him up another steep hill.

He stopped at a rocky plateau, leaving the trees behind, and turned to me. "Check this out."

I stepped toward the edge of the cliff.

Whoa.

The plateau overlooked the rest of the park. Hills and valleys stretched out below, covered in trees. I'd never seen a view like that before, so picturesque. For some reason, I always thought that scenery was something you like when you get old. But, man, it was kind of nice. I guess that meant I was getting old. Or maybe it's because we were together. I don't think seeing the scenery alone would have made me feel this way.

I looked to the sky. The sunset burned a little brighter from up here, painting the sky bright orange and deep blue.

This may be the last sunset I see, I thought. So I took it in.

As I watched the sun make the hills its grave, I started to reflect on things.

When I first woke up in 2008, I remember feeling lost and hopeless. It felt like each day that went by there was another day lost from my real life. All I cared about was getting back home. But then, at some point, something changed in me. I realized that even in a different world, my life was real and had meaning. And even though I was living in the past, I was still living. But not until a few people showed me how.

In the end, I think maybe the only difference between living and dying is the choice to try. The moment you give up, it's game over.

I don't know. Maybe that's a gross oversimplification.

But maybe it's not.

Maybe life doesn't have to be perfect for it to shine. Maybe it's the little moments that make our lives glow. Little moments like this.

"Come on," Ollie said, "let's go back before it gets dark."

"Okay," I said, not wanting to leave.

Before starting back down the trail, I looked over my shoulder at the view one last time, my mind wandering again.

That day, when I first stumbled into the laundromat, I didn't know how much my world would change.

But I'm glad it did.